Shen of the Sea

Shen of the Sea
Chinese Stories for Children

By *Arthur Bowie Chrisman*

Illustrated by Else Hasselriis

E. P. Dutton   New York

To V. T. S. this book is dedicated

Acknowledgment

I have heard
That the Plain of Fat Melons
Is more than flat.
It is hollowed like a bowl.
And my purse
Was quite as flat.
Then the *Philadelphia North American*,
And *What To Do*, of Elgin,
Bought some of my stories—
Paying good round money—
Which the baker was quick to take from me.
Furthermore,
These papers
Have given permission
To put the stories in a Book.
And the Book
Is open before you.
The *North American*,
And *What To Do*,
Have been as kind to me
As Wu Ta Lang was
To the red cherry tree.

Acknowledgment

And I thank them—
Not once—but twice—
And twice that—
More times than there are leaves
In Hu Pei Forest.

Contents

List of Illustrations

List of Illustrations

List of Illustrations

Shen of the Sea

Ah Mee's Invention

"A shamelessly rainy day, my honorable Brother Chi."

"That is truth, esteemed Brother Cha. It rains perfectly hard. There will be plenty of leisure in which to beat the children."

Ching Chi was merely quoting an old Swa Tou saying. Everyone knows that on rainy days old and young are crowded, arm against elbow, in the house; often to get in each the other's way—and misunderstandings are likely to arise. Then the bamboo is brought into play—and there are wailings. That is how the Swa Tou saying originated. When Ching Chi used it, he did so in fun, and, no doubt, to make talk.

But Ching Cha thought that his brother was speaking with earnestness. His face, made glum by the rain and by secret troubles, brightened at such a pleasing prospect. "Ho. Leisure to beat the children? What an utterly excellent idea! I myself will cut bamboos for your hand. Ah Mee is the one to beat. He played at being a mad wild elephant—oh, so perfectly wild, and with such trampling—in the midst of my *huang ya tsai* patch."

Ching Chi seemed altogether astonished. His face showed that he thought Ching Cha must be overstepping the truth. "What? What do you say to me, honorable Brother Cha? Ah Mee playing wild elephant in your cabbage patch? But I thought that I told him, emphatically, to break no more of your cabbages."

"It is no blemish upon my lips. It is the truth," said Ching Cha, sullen and hurt because Chi disbelieved. "He played elephant in my cabbages. Come and I will show you."

"Oh, no." Ching Chi shook his head. "It is raining far too hard. I'll speak of the matter again to my son."

Ching Cha adjusted his *wei li* (rain hat) the straighter and shuffled off through the downpour. As he went he muttered something that sounded like *"Wou tou meng."* If that is what he really said, he called Ching Chi a stupid old noddy.

But Ching Chi merely laughed. He had no intention of beating Ah Mee, his "pearl in the palm," his son.

Now, whether Ching Chi was right or wrong is a pretty question. Some persons answer in one way, and some, another. But there is no question about this. . . . Ah Mee was terrible. If anything, he was as bad as that lazy Ah Fun, son of Dr. Chu Ping. Here is their only difference: Ah Fun never did what he was told to do. Ah Mee always did what he was told *not* to do. But he did it in such manner as to leave a loophole. He always had a perfectly good excuse. Take the matter of his uncle Ching Cha's cabbage patch. . . .

Only a day or so before, Ah Mee had pretended that he was a fierce and furious dragon—a *loong*. As a fierce and furious dragon, he threshed this way and that through Uncle Ching Cha's very delectable cabbages—causing much hurt. Ching Chi, the parent, told Ah Mee never again to play dragon in Uncle Cha's cabbages. "Ah Mee, you must never again play dragon in your honorable uncle's cabbage patch. If you do, I shall speak to you most sharply." And Ah Mee said, "Yes, sir," and obeyed. He pretended to be a ferocious wild elephant. He didn't play dragon again. *Oh, no. Not at all. He was very careful not even to think of a dragon.* He was a weighty elephant—amid the cabbages.

Ching Chi, the fond parent, lived with his wife—

Oh, no. Not at all. He was very careful not even to think of a dragon. He was a weighty elephant—amid the cabbages.

her name is forgotten—and the son, Ah Mee, and a little daughter, in a neat house that stood in the Street of the Hill Where the Monkey Bit Mang. Ching Chi was a carver of wood and ivory and jade. His bachelor brother Ching Cha, who lived next door, did scrivening—wrote things with a blackened brush upon parchment and paper—and the wall, when he had no paper. Some people said they were stories, but certainly they brought in no money. As for that, neither did Ching Chi's carvings bring in any money. Yet Chi was a good carver. His designs were artistic, and his knife was obedient to the slightest touch. From an inch block of ivory he could carve seven balls—one inside another. Howbeit, Chi was neither famous nor wealthy. Instead of carving pagodas and trinkets for sale in the bazaars, he spent most of his time in carving toys for Ah Mee—who promptly smote them with an ax or threw them in the well or treated them in some other manner equally grievous.

For six months Ching Chi worked to carve a dragon. When finished, the *loong* was a thing of beauty. In the bazaar it would, perhaps, have fetched a bar of silver from some rich mandarin. But fond Ching Chi gave it to Ah Mee. And Ah Mee, tiring of it after five minutes of play, hurled it through the paper-covered window.

Are windows made to be broken? Are toys fashioned only to be thrown away? Certainly not. Papa Chi wagged a finger at Ah Mee and he spoke thus: "Ah Mee, most wonderful son in the world, you must not throw your dragon through the window into the back yard again. What I say, that I mean. Don't throw your dragon into the yard any more." Having said, he proceeded with his work, carving beautiful designs upon teakwood blocks . . . for Ah Mee's pleasure.

And Ah Mee said, "Very well then, *Tieh tieh*

[Daddy], I won't." He proceeded with his work—which was to pile carven teakwood blocks as high as his not-so-long arms could reach. There was one block covered with so much exquisite carving that it gave little support to the blocks above. For that reason the tower wavered and fell. Ah Mee promptly lost his temper. Made furious beyond endurance, he seized the offending block and hurled it through a paper-paneled door.

Who will say that Ah Mee was disobedient? He had been told not to throw his toy dragon through the window. But had his father, Ching Chi, told him not to heave a *block* through the *door*? Not at all. Ching Chi had said nothing about blocks, and he had pointed his finger at the window. Nevertheless, Mr. Ching felt almost inclined to scold his son. He said, very sternly, "Ah Mee . . ."

"Whang. Bang. Bang," came the sound of sticks on the doorframe. Crash—the door flew open. In rushed stalwart men, dressed in the King's livery, and bearing heavy staves. "Oh, you vile *tung hsi* [east west—very abusive talk], you murderer!" screamed the men. "Are you trying to assassinate your King? What do you mean by hurling missiles into the King's sedan as he is carried through the street? Answer, before your head falls!"

But Ching Chi was unable to answer. He could

only press his forehead to the floor, and tremble, and wait for the quick death he expected. Meanwhile, Ah Mee pelted the King's men with various large and small toys—including a hatchet.

King Tan Ki, seated comfortably in a sedan chair, was being carried through the Street of the Hill Where the Monkey Bit Mang. He had no thought of danger. Peril had no place in his mind. The street seemed a street of peace. When lo— from a paper-covered door there came a large missile, striking a slave and falling into the King's lap. Instantly the bodyguard rushed to the terrible house and battered in the door. But King Tan Ki felt more curiosity than alarm. He examined the object that had so unceremoniously been hurled into the sedan. At once his interest was quickened. The King knew good carvings—whether they came from old masters or from hands unknown. Here was a block carved with superlative art. Tan Ki wished to know more of the artist who carved it.

Ching Chi was still kneeling, still expecting instant death, when the King's Chamberlain rushed in. The Chamberlain uttered a sharp order. The bodyguards grasped Ching Chi and hastened him out of the house, to kneel at the King's sedan. Ah Mee fired a last volley of broken toys at the retreating Chamberlain. . . . Not especially nice of him, perhaps, but then, no one had forbidden it.

Fortune had smiled her prettiest upon the house of Ching Chi. King Tan Ki was immensely pleased with the old engraver's work. The odds and ends of toys that had been fashioned for Ah Mee now graced the palace. There they were appreciated. Every day Ching Chi worked faithfully, carving plaques and panels and medallions for the King. He was wealthy. Upon his little skullcap was a red button. He was a mandarin, if you please. Only mandarins of the highest class may wear ruby buttons on their caps. . . . And Ah Mee was worse than ever.

To say it again, for emphasis, Ah Mee was worse than ever—if possible. He dabbled in all the hundred-and-one varieties of mischief. All day long it was "Ah Mee, don't do that." "Ah Mee, don't do the other." "Don't. Don't. Don't." Papa Ching was so tired of saying "Don't" that his tongue hurt every time he used the word. Occasionally he changed his talk and said the opposite of what he really meant. Thus he would say, "That's right, little darling, fill Papa's boots with hoptoads and muddy terrapins, and that will make Papa happy." Or: "Pray take another jar, my precious. Eat all the jam you possibly can. Six jars is not at all too much." For Ah Mee doted on jam. It was a passion with him. He started the day on

jam, finished the day on jam. Every time a back
was turned, his fingers sought the jam pot. Indeed,
rather frequently he ate so much jam that there
were pains . . . and the doctor.

Ching Chi took a bird cage from the wall and
hung it on his arm. (In that land, when gentlemen
go for a stroll they usually carry their pet larks,
instead of their pet *chous*.) At the door he paused
and said to Ah Mee: "Little pearl in the palm,
please refrain from too much mischief. Don't
[there it was again] be any worse than you are
really compelled to be. Of course, it's quite proper
for you to put arsenic in Mother's tea, and to hit
baby sister with the ax again. And you may burn
the house if you feel so inclined. . . . I want you
to have plenty of innocent fun. But don't [again]
be bad. For instance, don't, I beg of you, don't get
in those jars of jam any more."

Off went Ching Chi with his lark singing
blithely.

Ah Mee was quite puzzled. "Don't get in the jars
of jam." How in the world *could* he get in the little
jars? It was silly. He was much larger than any
one of the jars. But perhaps *Tieh tieh* meant not
put a hand in the jars. That must be it. Ah Mee
made a stern resolve to keep his hands out. Not so
much as a finger should go in those jars. . . .

Obedient Ah Mee arranged several of his

father's carven plaques on the floor, and tilted a jar. The plaques were beautifully decorated flat pieces of wood, somewhat larger than dinner plates. They made reasonably good dishes for the stiff jam. Surrounded by little mountains of jam, Ah Mee sat on the floor and . . . how the mountains disappeared. Really, it was fairish-tasting jam.

When Ching Chi came home and discovered his carvings smeared with black and sticky jam, that good soul fell into a passion. First he screamed. Next he howled. *Then he seized the plaques and flung them from him,* flung them with all his strength. Flinging seems to have been a family failing.

Ching Chi was weeping for sorrow and howling with rage when his brother Cha entered the room. The quick eyes of Brother Cha soon saw that something was amiss. He gazed at the wall where the plaques had struck. He gazed at the jam-coated plaques. Then he too howled, but with joy. "Oh, Brother Chi," he shouted, "you have chanced upon a wonderful invention! It is a quick way for making books. What huge luck!" He led Brother Chi to the wall, and pointed. "See. For reason of its jam, each plaque has made a black impression on the wall. Every line of the carving is repro-

Then he seized the plaques and flung them from him.

duced upon the wall. Now do you understand? You will carve my thoroughly miserable stories upon blocks of wood. Ah Mee will spread black jam upon the carven blocks. Then I will press the blocks upon paper, sheet after sheet, perhaps a hundred in one day. . . . With the laborious brush I can make only one story a month. With the blocks—I can make thousands. Oh, what a wonderful invention!"

Ching Chi carved his brother's stories upon wooden blocks. Ah Mee spread the jam thickly—pausing only now and then for a taste. Ching Cha pressed the blocks upon paper, sheet after sheet. . . . There were the stories upon paper—all done in a twinkling, and with little expense. The poorest people in the land could afford to buy Ching Cha's most excellent stories.

Thus was invented *Yin Shu* (Make Books), or, as the very odd foreign demons call it in their so peculiar language—"Printing." Ching Chi, his brother Ching Cha, and Ah Mee all had a hand in the invention. As a matter of exact truth, Ah Mee had two hands in the invention (or in the jam), so he is generally given all the credit. His monument reads "Ah Mee, the Inventor of Printing."

Shen of the Sea

Kua Hai City stands on a plain in northern China. The plain is called Wa Tien, and it is very smooth and fertile, giving many large melons. . . . Life there is good. The plain is likewise extremely low. Any reliable geography will tell you that Kua Hai is below sea level. And that, I know, is a fact, for I, lazily seated in my garden, have often gazed at sailing ships, large-eyed—wide-staring-eyed junks as they fetched into the Bay of the Sharp-Horned Moon, and to view them I had to raise my eyes. It is very true. I had to look up, as one looks up to behold the sky-hung eagles of Lo Fan.

I had as often wondered if the sea ever broke through its restraining walls and flooded Kua Hai. A storm coming down from the northeast would most likely thrust billows to overtop the wall. So I said to my gardener, Wu Chang: "Wu Chang, did fishes ever swim up the Street of a Thousand Singing Dragons? Did the sea ever come into Kua Hai?" Wu Chang paused in his scratching among the *hung lo po* (the radishes). Since thinking it over, I am inclined to believe that he welcomed an opportunity to change from the working of his fingers to the working of his tongue. "Once, and once only, Honorable One, has the sea invaded Kua Hai. But it can never do so again. Chieh Chung was fooled once, but he was far too clever to be fooled twice. He buried the bottle, perhaps in this very garden, for who knows? He buried it so deep that no ordinary digging shall discover it. And so, the sea may look over the walls of Kua Hai, but it may not enter."

"Indeed?" said I. "And pray, who *was* this Chieh Chung? And what was in the bottle?"

Such astounding ignorance gained me a look of compassion from old Wu Chang. "The Honorable One is surely jesting. He of course knows that Chieh Chung was the first King of Wa Tien."

"Oh, to be sure," I interrupted. "It was Chieh Chung who invented—hum—er, radishes." That was a guess, and a miss.

Wu Chang corrected me. "Not radishes, but writing. A mistaken thing to do, in my opinion. But beyond doubt he did a great service when he bottled the water demons. Ho. Ho. Ho. He bottled the demons as if they were melon pickles. Ho. Ho. Ho."

"Sit here in the shade, Wu Chang," said I. "So Chieh Chung pickled the water demons—and then what?"

"Not pickled, Honorable One, bottled. Chieh Chung bottled the demons. Ho. Ho. Ho. . . . You must understand that in those days the plain hereabouts was much lower than it is now. It had not been built up. And the sea was much higher in those days, for then there were no heavy ships to weigh it down, and flatten it. The sea was very high then-a-days, far too high for its breadth. On every side the land held it back, and it was retarded and had no freedom of motion. So the Shen, the demons of the sea, got them together and took thought. They said: 'Our sea is far too small. We must have more room. We are mighty, are we not? Then let us take some land and occupy it, so that our sea may expand.'

"Accordingly, the water demons swam along the coast, seeking land to conquer. They passed the shores of Fu Sang without stopping, for that region is high and mountainous. They passed the region of San Shen Shan, for in that place lives the powerful land demon named Hu Kung. The water demons were in no great haste to gain Hu Kung's hatred. They passed without a second glance. But when the Shen swam up to Kua Hai, it was to rejoice. The demons looked over the wall; they smiled down upon Kua Hai, and said: 'This land we shall take for our beloved sea. It is low, and suited to our purpose. Rightfully it is ours. Yes, we shall take Kua Hai, and all the vast plain hereabout.' But the ocean demons were possessed of decency. They did not dash over the walls, calling on their sea to follow, and so drown all the people of Kua Hai. Demons though they be, the Shen that time had mercy in their hearts. While the night dew lay upon the fields of Wa Tien, those demons, to the number of seven, made their way into Kua Hai. There they waited in the garden of the palace.

"When King Chieh Chung, who ruled over Wa Tien, took him to the garden for an early-morning stroll, he discovered the demons waiting. He knew at once they were no ordinary men. Not once did they *kou tou* [knock their heads on the ground] as men should do. Nor did they look like the men of Wa Tien. Their mouths were wide mouths, like those of codfishes. Their bodies were covered with iridescent scales. Nevertheless, Chieh Chung permitted the Shen to approach. 'What manner of

We are the Shen, demons of the sea.

men are you?' asked the King. 'And what is your pleasure?'

" 'We are the Shen, demons of the sea,' answered the seven. 'We are Shen of the ocean, and we come to claim our own.' 'And what is that?' asked the King, smiling tolerantly upon them, though in truth he felt more like weeping, for he knew what would be the answer.

" 'We have come to possess ourselves of the city and all the low plain that surrounds it. It is our right, and our might—we mean to have it.' Then Chieh Chung's heart dropped down to a level with his sandals. His heart was weighted as if with millstones, as if weighted with Mount Tai. Long he stroked his beard, pondering, grieving, praying. And the water demons danced in the dew. Jubilant were they, flinging their toes high, spattering dewdrops upon the palace roof, and singing the terrible song of the ocean.

"Finally the King answered. 'Shen,' said he, 'what time do you grant me? Kua Hai is a large city. In it are half a million souls. It will be moons and moons before I can count my people safely upon the Mountain of the Yellow Ox.' One of the demons was shaking a *pai shu* [cypress tree] so that its dew fell upon him and upon his companions, for already the sun was up and they were beginning to feel the day and its dryness. 'What time?' said the Shen, taking his answer from the *pai shu*. 'We shall give you until this tree is in flower. Have all your people gathered upon high ground when this *pai shu* blossoms, for at that time we shall lead the sea upon Wa Tien, and the sea shall stand three *li* deep above your palace. That is our answer. And now we must go, for the sun has lit his fire.'

"The Shen made a move as if to depart, but no sooner were they out of the shadows than they halted abruptly, murmuring in displeasure. And small wonder. The sun had dispelled the dew, and there was no moisture upon the land. A water Shen cannot exist where there is no moisture. In that respect he is like the *yin yu* and the *shih pan* [fishes]. So the Shen turned to Chieh Chung and said, 'Is there water here, O King, where we may spend the day hours?' 'There is little,' said Chieh Chung; 'I dare say too little for your purpose. But in such quantity as it is, you are welcome.' He pointed to a crystal bowl in which burgeoned a sacred lily. There was water in the bowl, water surrounding the lily bulb. Too, there were stones in the bowl—blue lapis lazuli, and green jade, and yellow topaz (precious stones, as befitted a palace garden), for that is the way sacred lilies are grown

—in bowls filled with water and pretty pebbles. 'You are quite welcome to it,' reiterated the King. The Shen shook their heads half in despair. 'It is too little,' groaned they, 'far too little.' 'But,' said Chieh Chung, 'you are demons—hence magicians. Why do you not make yourselves smaller? Why not change yourselves into red *hung pao shih* and recline in the bowl amid the lily roots? I am sure you would make handsome rubies. Beyond a doubt, my courtiers would say ''Ah'' and ''How lovely,'' and admire you greatly when they saw you. Of a certainty, you would make resplendent gems, dazzling and superb.' 'Well,' agreed the Shen, somewhat dubiously, 'we shall try it. If you have no more water, it is the only thing we *can* do.' And so, in a twinkling the Shen were gone, and seven beautiful rubies appeared in the crystal bowl.

'' 'How lovely,' said Chieh Chung—and deliberately winked at the cypress tree, first with one eye and then with the other. He went to a cabinet that stood in his chamber, and from the cabinet took a bottle fashioned out of *fei yu* [a cloudy jade]. And the bottle had a wide mouth. Into it Chieh Chung poured water. Returning to the lily bowl, he quickly took therefrom the seven red *hung pao shih* and dropped them into the jade bottle—closing the mouth securely.

" 'Now,' exulted the King, 'my city is saved. My people may walk in security and without fear. The seven water demons are in my keeping, and please Heaven may they never escape my hand.' And in his joy, King Chieh Chung ordered that ten thousand catties of rice be given to the poor.

"Weeks lengthened into months. Lengthened the months to years. Still languished the water demons in the clouded jade bottle. Still broke the sea on Kua Hai's walls—but did not enter. Chieh Chung added to his kingdom, and ruled with beneficence. His name was heralded throughout the length of the world. Not by the spear, but by wisdom he added to his dominions. Peoples of far-distant regions came seeking to place themselves under the rule of Chieh Chung—wisest and best.

"At length came ambassadors from Wei Chou, yes, even from distant Kou Pei, offering to give their allegiance to Chieh Chung. Ah, but that was a great day, a day of all proud days. The ambassadors were a hundred for number, haughty mandarins all. There was a great stir about the palace, you may well believe, retainers rushing hither and thither to provide food and drink and entertainment for the foreign great men.

"A foolish servant, ransacking cupboard and closet for what victuals and drink he could find, came upon the dusty jade bottle that stood in Chieh Chung's cabinet. 'Ah,' said the servant, trying to peer through the cloudy jade. 'Beyond a doubt, here is something of rare excellence. This will do for the highest of the mandarins, for the red-button mandarins with peacock feathers. It rattles—rock candy in it.' And the foolish one removed the stopper. A thousand pities he was not stricken dead before the seal was broken.

"Chieh Chung came into the chamber and saw what had happened. For a moment he was stunned. Then, 'Let me have the bottle.' The bottle was empty, all save for a bit of water. 'They are gone,' said the King. 'The Shen have escaped. But even so, I may baffle them, for they promised with binding oaths not to take my kingdom until the *pai shu* blossoms. And in this region the cypress tree never blossoms—it *never* comes into flower.' The King smiled in spite of himself.

"Meanwhile, the water demons, having escaped from the bottle, hastened through the palace toward the garden. They were very angry, were those demons, gnashing their teeth with a noise like that of waves lashing a rock-guarded coast. They were determined on vengeance.

"The Wei Chou ambassadors were encamped in the palace garden. Their servants had been washing garments, brilliant-hued garments such as the wealthy and noble of that land wear. The garments had been hung on the cypress tree to dry. And there the garments hung when the water demons appeared. The tree was aflame with color. Instantly the Shen raised a great shout: 'Come billow! Come ocean!' They shouted in triumph. 'The *pai shu* blossoms [the cypress tree blooms]'—for they thought the garments were flowers—'and our promise is ended. Kua Hai is ours.'

"Fathoms deep, roaring, grinding, relentless, the sea swept over Kua Hai, buried the city, buried the plain. The water demons raced before it, calling it on. They who had been the people of Kua Hai rode upon white-crested billows—without life —drowned. Out of all the vast population perhaps a thousand escaped. And among those who escaped was the King.

"Chieh Chung sat under a pine tree on the mountain, grief-stricken, heartbroken, gazing upon what had been a city and now was sparkling sea. Hour after hour sat the King, grieving and thinking, meditating a way to regain his country. Now and then the seven water demons appeared before him, mocking, splashing him with spray.

"One day, having meditated long, Chieh Chung arose and shouted exultantly: 'I have it! I know how I shall regain my city. I shall go immediately and put the plan in writing, while it is fresh in my mind.' Having said, he walked to the little hut that served for his palace, and sat down at a table to write. On the table stood a crystal bowl, with a lily, and with green, blue, and yellow stones.

"Chieh Chung sat writing meaningless stuff upon parchment. All the while he kept an eye on the crystal bowl. Lo. There appeared seven red stones at the root of the lily. The demons had come to spy upon the King's writing. They had come to learn his plan, and so triumph over him. But they, unwittingly, were giving themselves into bondage again. For Chieh Chung quickly thrust them into a bottle and sealed it against all escape. Six of the demons he thus imprisoned. The seventh, who was a small fellow, Chieh Chung threw back into the sea. 'Go,' said the King, 'and take your sea with you. Take your sea, and never trouble me again. Else I shall most certainly destroy your six brothers. It is a warning.'

"So the seventh demon sped away, taking the sea with him. Then did Chieh Chung descend to Kua Hai and build up the city, people coming in from far countries. Once more the city was inhabited, and the land was richer, by reason of its flooding.

So the seventh demon sped away, taking the sea with him.

"And the six Shen, the six water demons, are buried deep, in a jade bottle—perhaps under this very garden."

How Wise Were the Old Men

With the first splash of ink it should be stated that this, the story of Meng Hu, is not intended for those who disbelieve in signs and portents. Such persons will merely say "Pish" and "Tush," together with other hurtful remarks, and remain unconvinced and scornful. But the open-minded—they are the people. They will nod their heads in understanding.

So. The history of Meng Hu, a merry rascal, and a clever.

Upon the night that Meng Hu was born, in the house of his father, Hao Shou, in the village named Two Roads Meeting, which stands at the foot of Mount Chieh Man (meaning: "Do not hurry—it is tremendously steep"), in Ping Shan Province, there happened many queer and unseemly happenings. A pack of wolves came down from Mount Chieh Man, and, leaping into Hao Shou's pigsty, carried off a well-fattened red-and-black pig, for which Hao Shou had been offered eighty cash—every one good. Between the howling of the wolves and the squealing of the red-and-black pig, all Two Roads Meeting Village was aroused.

The excitement had scarcely subsided when Hao Shou's pet monkey, for some reason best known to himself and the Shen of mischief, entered the house where Hao Shou's fowls roosted. The disturbance thus created caused Two Roads Meeting Village again to leap from bed.

Only an hour later a tiger, which some coolies were carrying as a gift to the King, escaped from his cage, and with much roaring pounced upon Hao Shou's amiable white cow. There was no more sleep in Two Roads Meeting Village that night. And no wonder.

Now, the village called Two Roads Meeting was much like any other village, in that it housed some extremely wise men—men who knew everything about practically everything. These men gathered, and wagged their beards much. Some of them said: "It is a sign, an omen. Hao Shou's son, born in the midst of last night's disturbances, will gain his fortune by the agency of animals. With the help of animals, he undoubtedly will become King. . . . He may even become mayor of our excellent village." Other wise men, however, said to the first: "Do you fellows live in a well? [You don't know much of the world.] To be sure it is an omen—but *mei chi* [a bad one]. The son of Hao Shou will be done to death by animals. Mark our words." Then the old men of the two parties fell to fighting, and forgot all about Meng Hu, son of Hao Shou, the innocent cause.

Having lost his pig, his cow, and many of his fowls, the father of Meng Hu found himself a pauper. He who had been rich was now poor. Worse still, a suit was brought by the tiger's owner. The great beast had been gored while pulling down Hao Shou's sinful white cow, and its owner sued in a court for damages. Being unable to pay, Hao Shou went to jail—and lucky he was to escape with his miserable life. For the tiger was being sent, a gift, to the King.

Thus beset by poverty, the boy Meng Hu was no sooner able to walk than he was bound over to a herder, who immediately put him to work. It was

Meng Hu's duty to watch over a flock. Early every morning he drove his sheep into the green hills, watching over them throughout the day, and with night's coming, marshaled them back to the lowland fold. It was lonesome work, very. Meng Hu had no companions with whom to play and chatter. The solitude oppressed him. He sometimes thought that his mind must surely break—insanity would claim him. A flute, such as the other shepherds used to beguile away loneliness, was beyond his means to buy. But he must have something, must do something.

While thinking of a plan to amuse, he became aware that he was making strange noises in his throat. He opened his mouth. A long, weird howl echoed between the hills. It was the howl of a wolf—yet it came from the throat of Meng Hu. It came without effort: a perfect wolf cry. The boy was quite as surprised as were his sheep. He went away from the flock to a secluded valley, where he could practice the cry without harm. "Ow-w-w-w-wh," and again "Ow-w-w-w-wh." The sound was terrifying. Any gray leader of a pack might have been proud of it.

At last Meng Hu grew tired of making wolf howls. He tried his voice at imitating the calls of other animals. A cow—"Am-oo-ooh." Sun-awaken-ing rooster—"Cockadoodledoo." A tiger: Meng Hu gave the buzzing sound of pleasure, the open-mouthed roar of anger, the coughing "woof" of pain. He found it easy to give the various calls of *hou erh* (the monkey). He squealed in a manner most pig-like. He imitated the "Onkee Onkee" of his master's donkey. He gave the neigh of a horse.

Day after day Meng Hu practiced in the hills, imitating the calls of many animals, usually in a low voice so that his sheep would receive no fright.

It was the howl of a wolf.

46

Lonesomeness no longer oppressed him. He had a toy more entrancing than a lute with ivory bands. He was wolf and tiger and clucking biddy by turns. He knew all cries of the wild.

A train of coolies trudged along the road below. Meng Hu, seeing them, thought to have great fun. He placed his hands trumpet fashion to his mouth and gave the wolves' hunting song: "Ow-w-w-w-wh." Instantly the coolies flung down their burdens and ran as fast as men can run to the village. Those scary fellows had no wish to help fatten a famine-maddened wolf. Naturally, their fright lent great powers to their imaginations. Not only had they heard the wolf—they had seen him—as large as the Emperor's battle horse. And the flock owners had better see about their sheep. A dozen sheep would be only a trifling morsel for that huge beast. This large—holding their hands high in air.

How the village hubbubbed with excitement! Such a collection of spears and scythes and warlike jingals as rushed to the wolf-haunted hills!

When Meng Hu saw half of the village's population drawing near in a glorious gleam of weapons, he realized what had happened. Beyond a doubt, he would be questioned. Had he seen the wolf? They would ask him that. No—he hadn't *seen* the wolf, but most certainly he had heard it. Perhaps the beast was hiding in the thicket. Then hunt for it. That would prevent suspicion.

The villagers came up, to find Meng Hu bravely poking with his staff in the bushes. Oh, but they praised him. "See," said the villagers, "brave Meng Hu all alone hunts the wolf. How courageous is Meng Hu. His heart is as bold as the heart of Mi Tze—he who pulled the King's beard. Valiant Meng Hu is an added honor to the Village of Two Roads Meeting—renowned for its heroic men."

Meng Hu said nothing—just then. When alone, he brayed like a donkey. It was so funny, so laughably ridiculous. He had fooled the wisest men of Two Roads Meeting Village.

For the next several days Meng gave the villagers plenty of violent exercise. He had them come puffing up the hill at all hours. "Ow-w-w-w-w-w-wh." One long-drawn-out howl was sufficient to set scythes and spears in motion.

But the villagers were not so gullible as one might think. They had eyes. Why was it that they never *saw* the wolf? Never a glimpse could they catch of the rogue. And there were no tracks to be found. Suspicion dawned. Could it be that someone was making sport of Two Roads Meeting Village? Several men hid in the bushes. Meng Hu was seen to climb a rock that overhung the lowland. He raised his hands to form a trumpet. "Ow-w-w-w-wh." The wolf.

"Oho," said the men, of whom the flock owner was one. "Aha. So it was you all the time." They rushed upon Meng Hu and gave him a good taste of bamboo sauce, which is served upon the back, and sounds "Swish, thump. Swish, thump." The flock owner then paid Meng what few cash were due and bade him, *"Chu pa* [Away with you]. And don't dare ever to return. *Hsiao tsai tzu* [You young animal]."

Meng Hu called to his heels for assistance. He ran and ran, till the hills were far behind. Every now and again he murmured sadly: "How wise were the old men! They *said* that an animal would be my downfall. A wolf. A mock wolf was my undoing."

The lowland was a pleasant country, with here and there a ripening field, and here and there a forest. Young Meng stood at the edge of a wood, casting about for a bed to serve him the night. A clatter of hoofs broke the silence. Some twenty men or more dashed into view. From their weapons and general swashbuckling appearance Meng knew them to be robbers. And knowing—he swiftly clambered up a tree.

The robbers halted and gazed about them right and left. Their chieftain said: "I thought I saw a man here. If you find him, kill him, for the people hereabouts are fierce enemies. Ho . . . WHAT'S THAT IN YONDER LEAFY TREE?"

Meng Hu could imagine a knife at his throat. He shook the tree with his trembling. Nevertheless, his wits worked faithfully. From his lips came the scolding chatter of *hou erh* (the monkey). It was exceedingly well done. The robber chieftain laughed. "Only a monkey—and what vile names he seems to call us! Ho. Ho. Ho. Only a silly monkey."

Meng Hu tossed down a ripened fruit from the tree—that being the way of all monkeys. The fruit spattered its juices in the chieftain's eyes. "What a sweet-tempered old brute!" complained the chief. "Hurry on. We've no time to waste with a monkey."

The robbers rode deeper into the forest, and under a spreading tree dismounted. Meng Hu, now feeling that he was a match for forty robbers, followed the trail and spied upon the camp. He saw the knaves divide their booty—gold and jewels flashing in the firelight. There were bales of rich silk, brocades and moires—all rich stuffs. The eyes of Meng popped with amazement. He wished that

Meng Hu could imagine a knife at his throat.

someday he might own such treasure. But why not own it at once—why wait for *some* day? Could there be any way to take it from the robbers? He shut his dazzled eyes, and thought.

The night was at its most eerie hour—the hour when whitened ghosts appear—when the *yao mo* (the ghosts that have no chins) appear. A monkey chattered in frantic warning. The robber chief awoke and said to his men: "Do you hear that sound? Monkeys always make such alarm when danger is near. That monkey warns us—a tiger is near. Get to your horses."

Before the thieves could mount their horses, the horror-striking, the flesh-chilling roar of a tiger filled the forest. Instantly the horses dashed away. Shrieking with fear, the brigands followed. Three roars emptied the camp. Six roars emptied the forest. Between roars Meng Hu found breath enough to murmur: "How wise were the old men of the village! They *said* that an animal would bring me my fortune. A tiger. A pretty tiger am I. Ho. Ho. Ho." And he roared again for good measure.

Morning's glow was still faint in the east when Meng rounded up the horses. Those that had strayed too far he ignored. No telling when the robbers would return. Besides, the boy had plenty, in all conscience. As blithe as any bobolink, he bobbed up and down, pounding the road toward Chang An, the capital city.

The fortunate fellow settled down in a comfortable mansion, and converted his goods into gold as rapidly as possible. To put the merchants in better humor and make them more disposed to buy his silks and jewels, Meng Hu often howled and mooed and cackled. He gave the buyers much entertainment. His strange antics became the talk of Chang An City.

The upshot was that Lui Tsung, Mightiest King, heard of the youth who made such marvelous noises. His Majesty sent a courier, bidding Meng Hu appear in the square that fronted the palace, there to entertain. Meng promptly appeared, bringing with him a tiger robe, a calfskin, a wolf hide, and other disguises. He intended that the performance should seem very real. And so it was, at first. As a wolf, he frightened three soldiers into running. His bawling was so true to life that an old peasant rushed to the square, declaring that he recognized the voice of his lost calf, and would someone lend him a rope? Oddly enough, the tiger mimicry created no astonishment. It caused neither laughs nor screams. Meng Hu was surprised. Had he not thrown fear into the robbers' very marrow with his tiger noise? Roaring furiously, he rushed at a soldier. The soldier merely yawned. Roaring ten times more furiously, the "tiger" sprang at Lui Tsung, the Mighty King. . . .

Now, of course, Meng Hu was merely a peasant boy. He knew nothing of royalty and its ways. But is ignorance ever an excuse? Never. Meng Hu should have known better than to spring at his Monarch, and to tooth the royal robes. His Majesty gasped, and beckoned to a captain of the guard. "Seize this audacious person and imprison him. Hold him until I can think of an utterly new punishment to fit his crime. He merits something more severe than mere sword or fire."

With such delightful prospects to ponder, Meng Hu languished behind lock and key. Over and over he moaned: "How wise were the old men! They *said* that I would meet my death because of an animal. A tiger. A tiger. *Ai ja* [Alas]." Though extremely downcast, yet he kept a faint hope. His mind fabricated numerous schemes for escape. He had noticed that the Queen seemed extremely fond of a ridiculous little yipping Chou. (The scamp: with his noise he had frightened the poor dog in a manner most scandalous.) While thinking of the Chou, he hit upon an idea that promised much.

Directly after the new guards had been posted,

Meng Hu began to yelp dismally. His yelping was enough to bring tears of pity to the soldiers' eyes. It was distressing. Presently a voice said: "O soldiers, my dear little dog is locked up, and I don't know where. Hasten and open all the doors." That voice was the Queen's voice. Every soldier of the guard recognized it. Every soldier hastened along the corridor—slip slap, slip slap—opening doors. One and all they hastened to free the Queen's dear little pet Chou.

The Queen's voice commanded that the doors be opened. Yet, at that very moment the Queen was in a sedan chair, several miles away, taking her evening ride. Perhaps Meng Hu could have explained the mystery—had he waited. But there was no waiting. The guards had not finished opening the farther doors when Meng crawled away. He didn't even pause to thank the guards. Their kindness went unrewarded.

To the wall. To the gate. Toward the Great Wall galloped Meng Hu. The night cloaked his hurry. No one hindered. No one pursued. Over the mountain—a mile to go. There stood the Great Wall— there the gate. There lay safety.

Meng paused for a breath and turned in his saddle. Far behind appeared a streak of light. That would be a torch—and a King's man bearing it. They were pursuing—upon the King's swift horses. Then hasten. Speed. To the gate.

Away galloped Meng Hu. . . . The gate was before him. . . . Closed . . . Closed. *Ai ja*. His escape was blocked by the ponderous gate. He would be captured. He would be killed, and alas for it. *Ai ja*. The gate was closed for the night. It would not be opened till morning came. No ten bags of gold could open it before the morning dawned. Not even a royal order could open it.

The warden of the gate slept peacefully.

"Cockadoodledoo."

The warden turned in his quilt.

"Cockadoodledoo."

The warden opened his eyes. "Can it be so late?"

"Cockadoodledoo."

"Heigho. Morning already—and—what a noisy fowl!"

"Cockadoodledoo."

"Yes, it must be morning. Time to open the gate, so that the early caravans can pass."

"COCKADOODLEDOO."

The key clicked in the lock. The heavy hinges groaned.

Clatter, clatter of hoofs that were urged.

"How wise were the old men of the village!"

murmured Meng Hu. "They *said* that an animal would save my neck someday. A rooster. What a toothsome fowl am I ! Ho. Ho. Ho."

He laughed as his horse took the open road.

Chop-Sticks

What is better than roast duck with sweet ginger dressing? Is anything—anything—in the world and all, superior? Two roast ducks—as Ching Chung said—are more to be desired? Ah, of a certainty. Two. Two roast ducks, with *hong keong* dressing, and *ling gow,* and *jung yee,* and *tou ya,* and *yu chien* (the very fine tea that grows only in three gardens of Ku Miao), and—but really that's enough for any dinner. More might mean misery.

Those were the dishes that Cheng Chang prepared with matchless perfection. Those were the dishes that Ching Chung ate with the utmost gusto.

Cheng Chang, the very fine cook, and Ching Chung, the extremely appreciative master. They were old bachelors, those two worthies. Little Cheng Chang and large Ching Chung were foot-free, funny, and forty. Cheng Chang came within an inch of being a dwarf. He was only a mere trifle taller than his own willow-wood ladle. Why, he was nearly as short as Wu Ta Lang, who, as you'll remember, when standing under his cherry tree could not reach the limb, and when on the limb could not touch earth.

Beyond a doubt, Cheng Chang was little—but . . . how he could cook! He was ugly—but . . . how he could cook! He tied his queue with a leather string—but . . . how he could cook! He taught his own grandmother how to roast eggs— and that's something few men could do.

Ching Chung was the master. He was a tremendous person. He was nearly as large as Ho Lan, the giant, who, one day when stretching, burned his hand on the hot red sun. Surely no one could ask for more proof that Ching Chung was quite large. And how the man could eat! He worked hard, from crow of cock till the owl said "Time for bed." And how he could eat! Four roast ducks at a sitting . . . how he could eat! But his voice was so powerful that it often shook the pots from Cheng

Chang's stove. Then there was nothing to eat.

Ching Chung frequently complimented Cheng Chang upon his so glorious cookery. He would say to Cheng Chang: "Cheng Chang, this roast duck is simply *tou ming*. If I were King and you my cook, I would make you Governor of Kwang Ting, where the best ducks grow." And Cheng Chang would say: "To the Gracious Master I offer my no-account thanks. I sorrow that my terrible cooking is not better." Or, again, Ching Chung would say: "Cheng Chang, this exquisite roast duck has infused me with new strength. One more morsel, or maybe two, and I could conquer the world." And Cheng Chang would reply, "It is nothing, Honorable Master."

Strengthened and made bold by Cheng Chang's roast duck and perhaps by a sip of the stuff called *sam shu* (which is fire and madness in a bottle), Ching Chung one day went a-courting. Before a body could say *"Chang wang li chao"* (about the same as "Jack Robinson"), the beauteous lady Li Kuan was pledged to be Ching Chung's bride. Whereat, the happy groom-to-be, who had always proclaimed that a bachelor's life was the only life, promptly changed the burden of his song and declared that all old bachelors should be boiled in rancid bean oil and used as candles to lighten the darkness. And, no doubt, he was very right.

Said master to cook: "Cheng Chang, why don't you follow the excellent example that I have set and take unto yourself a bride? There's Pang Tzu, a buxom lady, and wealthy. Why not marry Pang Tzu?" So Cheng Chang answered, "Very well then, Honorable Master; I'll do as you advise." And he did.

With Ching Chung married and Cheng Chang wed, both of the old bachelors were husbands, and their lives were changed, utterly. For marriage is a most peculiar thing. It promotes the fortunes of some men. Other men go from bad to worse. The wedding bell has two tongues. One tongue speaks good; the other, evil.

Consider the case of Ching Chung. His wife had no wealth whatsoever. But her fifth cousin was a general in the royal army. The general came to visit, riding a handsome donkey, and wearing his two swords. He tasted the roast duck (cooked, mind you, by Cheng Chang), upon Ching Chung's table, and instantly took a great liking for Ching Chung. He thought his host a most hospitable and excellent man. Nor was he wrong. (But Cheng Chang had cooked the duck.)

It was no time till Ching Chung received a commission in the royal and brave army. He became a general. Before one could say *"Chang wang li chao,"* he won a great victory. . . . And, the King having died meanwhile, Ching Chung was placed upon the throne. There he was—upon the throne— a King. And hail to King Ching Chung.

On the other hand, consider Cheng Chang, the cook. Poor Cheng Chang. He was afraid of his wife. Horribly afraid. His wife had but to whisper "Chang," and Chang trembled like jelly, spilled on the King's highroad. His wife had but to say "Cheng Chang," and Cheng Chang fell upon the floor. It often happened that his wife said "Chang," just as the poor man seasoned a duck on the stove. Then Cheng Chang would tremble, and drop in too much salt or garlic or ginger, and the dinner would be ruined. Frequently Cheng Chang had to throw away a dozen ducks before he dished up one that was really excellent. Of course, his own purse had to pay for the loss. Almost before one could say *"Chang wang li chao,"* the timid Cheng Chang was a pauper. A lucky thing for him that his wages were raised as soon as Ching Chung became King.

How remarkable are the tricks played by Fate! She gives the wheel of life a turn. What was top becomes bottom. Strangly enough, what was bottom—becomes top. The once mighty eat humble pie. The once lowly sit upon gilt chairs, drinking *yu chien* from cups of eggshell porcelain, and eating birds' nests. Cheng Chang was at the bottom. And Fate gave the wheel a whirl.

The wife of Cheng Chang went to visit her three brothers, who conducted a large godown in Ning Poo. The art of cookery, so nearly lost to Cheng Chang, once more thrilled in his finger tips. A pinch of this. A mite of that. A dash of something else. Cheng Chang cooked as he had never cooked before. The roast duck that he served up for King Ching Chung was—was—was— There are many words in the language of men, but not one of them can describe the duck that Cheng Chang presented his King and master, Ching Chung. Sublime, delicious, perfect—those words are weak and unable. Away with them! The duck must remain undescribed. But, oh, what a duck it was! King Ching Chung ate half of it. Perhaps he ate a trifle more than half. He kept his gaze upon the platter. He said neither "Good," nor "Bad."

Cheng Chang lingered near by to receive the praise that he felt was due. But the praise was slow in forthcoming. The wondering cook began to fear that he had dropped in too much *chiao fen*. Horrors. Horrors twice. Suppose he had? He deserved to be killed.

King Ching Chung laid his knife aside. He placed his fork in company. He raised his eyes and gazed at Cheng Chang. For a full minute he gazed. He questioned, "Cheng Chang, did you cook this duck?" Poor Cheng Chang. Down he went, kneeling three times. Each time he knelt, his head rapped the floor thrice. "Yes, most gracious and forgiving Majesty, I cooked the duck. I, Cheng Chang, alone am guilty. Oh, have mercy." He could almost feel the headsman's sword.

Steadily for another minute the Monarch stared. Then he spoke. "You did, did you? Well, all I can say is this. The man who cooked this duck should be King. And, by the teeth of the bobtailed dragon who brings famine, I am going to make him King. I shall abdicate and appoint him to rule in my stead. Arise, King Cheng Chang, ruler of the universe—and the best cook that ever roasted a duck.

As soon as Cheng Chang's wife heard of her smaller half's good fortune, she hurried back to the palace. With her she fetched the three brothers, feeling sure that King Cheng Chang would appoint them to high places. If he wouldn't, *she* would. She had things planned to the last detail. One brother was to be Keeper of the royal and full treasury. What a clever idea! He had the largest

pockets. Another brother was to be Governor of
Kwang Ting. The third was to be made Com-
mander-in-Chief of the royal and never-run army.

At breakfast, the eldest brother mentioned his
desire. "Oh," said King Cheng Chang, "I can't
make you Keeper of the treasury. I've already put
in a man who has no hands." "Well, what appoint-
ment have you saved for me?" "For you? Let's
see. You can be Ambassador to Ho Chung Kuo."
(A far-off country—America, in fact.) "Indeed?"
screamed the Queen's brother in terrible rage. He
took his knife from his mouth and lunged at the
King. . . . Only a remarkable quickness of foot
saved King Cheng Chang.

His Majesty, very properly, was much dis-
pleased at such unseemly behavior. Who wouldn't
be? "I shall have your eldest brother beheaded,"
he told the Queen. "Indeed?" said the Queen.
"Then I shall beat you." So that ended that. He
was little and she was large. There was no be-
heading.

At dinner the Queen's second brother remarked
in a casual tone: "It's an exquisite day, isn't it? I
hope it will be this pleasant when I am inaugu-
rated Governor of Kwang Ting." "You? Governor? I have appointed Ching Chung to be Governor of Kwang Ting. You can be constable at—"

"Indeed?" screamed the would-be governor in an ungovernable rage. He seized his fork and rushed at the King. Fortunately, a mat slipped from beneath his feet. His fork tore a deep furrow in the floor. The Monarch escaped injury.

Nevertheless, King Cheng Chang was highly indignant. Surely that was his kingly right. He said to the Queen, "I shall have your brother be—" The Queen interrupted, "If you do, I shall beat you." She rather had him there. The King crawled under his throne. The subject was closed, and the headsman's sword was unstained.

Supper had barely begun when the Queen's youngest brother, a huge brawny yokel, remarked that he had already purchased his uniform and would take over the army tomorrow. The King was taken aback. "You command the army? Huh. I shall make you Minister to Yin Yung." (A place twenty thousand li distant as the ships sail.) "Indeed?" roared the Queen's brawny youngest brother. Clutching his soup spoon, he leaned across the table and struck at King Cheng Chang, "Swish," with all his might.

Thanks to him who made the table, he made it of generous width. The Queen's youngest brother could not quite reach across it. His murderous spoon merely parted the King's beard. It was a

The King crawled under his throne.

most atrocious deed, meriting extreme punishment, but it caused no actual pain. Its main effect was upon the King's dignity. But this time His Royal Mightiness said nothing of the headsman. He imagined that his wife would most likely raise objections. No. The King said nothing of punishment. Instead, he rewarded the Queen's youngest brother, appointed him director of the Imperial Gunpowder Factory, with a bed in the factory. . . . And gave him six pounds of smoking tobacco.

The three attempts upon his life worked havoc with Cheng Chang's nerves. When eating breakfast, he could never look at a knife without shuddering. Seated at dinner, each time he touched a fork cold chills raced down his marrow. At supper, he could scarcely eat because of the spoon. Each glance at the spoon wrung from His Majesty a groan of dread.

So King Cheng Chang did a most wise thing. He abolished knives and forks and spoons. He ate his rice and duck with the aid of two harmless, delicate little sticks. There was nothing about the sticks to inspire uneasiness. They were incapable of hurt.

The little sticks used by King Cheng Chang were called Chop-Sticks. Chop means "good."

Naturally enough, all the people in Cheng

Chang's kingdom soon were using chop-sticks. They wished to do as the King did. People are like that. Chop-sticks became, first, fashionable, then, universal. Everyone used them.

Wherefore, today King Cheng Chang is remembered, not for his roast duck—which was heavenly, and gained him the throne—but for his chop-sticks which are wood, mere wood.

Buy a Father

The Street of Wang's Broken Tea Cup lies between Seven Thieves Market and the long wharf where ship bottoms from all the world (and, as some say, the moon) discharge their varied cargoes. Queer sights are so excessively common there that the phoenix bird lighting a match to his feathers would, probably, excite only ordinary interest. Nevertheless, the people *do* possess eyes, and they *are* provided with ears. Now and again they can be made to open those eyes, and sharpen those ears into eager hearing. The ridiculous, in especial, rouses their attention. There was the wit-wandering beggar, Weng Fu, as an instance.

Weng Fu walked in the Street of Wang's Broken Tea Cup, bearing a great bundle of bamboo switches upon his back, and shouting thunderously: "Who'll buy? Who'll buy? What young man wishes to buy him a father?" Whereat, several persons gathered, laughing. "I, Weng Fu, will sell myself as a father to any young man for only five cash." The crowd and the laughter increased. "Who'll buy a pretty father? An orphan may have me for only one cash. A most excellent father I'll be to my son. I promise to beat him twice each day. Of every hundred cash he earns I'll take only ninety-nine, and he may keep one. I'll even let him sleep upon warm ashes in the bed-stove. Ho— young men, come buy—come buy."

The shopkeepers left their stalls unguarded as they gathered round Weng Fu to mock and express their not-flattering opinions. "Surely," said they, "this is the oddest fellow we have had in a long while. He must think our young men are as silly as Ko Chih, who scrabbled in the deep snow of January, searching for plums. Ho. Ho. Ho. Was there ever anything more ridiculous? A pretty father he would make. Pretty indeed." A crowd of boys assembled to have sport with the fantastic beggar. "Here, most honorable Father—here is five cash, and I will be your dutiful son." A richly dressed youth held out some money to Weng Fu. But when Weng Fu grabbed at it, the boy shut his hand and ran away swiftly, cackling in well-pleased laughter. After him plunged the greedy beggar, his tattered clothing flapping like strings on a scarecrow. A bystander put out a foot. The old man tripped heels over head in the deep black mud. Then the crowd slip-slapped on, mildly interested in a fight between Wan the hunchback who had only one leg, and a blackamoor who had no arms.

The boy Ah Tzu, an orphan, approached Weng and tugged to assist him. The beggar's rags tore away by the handful. A train of laden donkeys labored down the street. "Ho. Good man, you must get out of this," shouted Ah Tzu, pulling. "The donkeys will shred your flesh from the bones. Come." "Will you buy me for a father?" "Certainly. Now see if you cannot arise." Ah Tzu pulled manfully, and the contrary old beggar moved his limbs in helping. The two staggered aside just in time to avoid being trampled. "Where shall we go—Father—where is your house?" asked Ah Tzu. "In the Street of the Place Where the Cow Lost Her Horn," answered Weng Fu. "And don't walk so fast, my son, else I shall beat you."

The house of Weng Fu was luxurious in the extreme. A goat could have leaped through any one of a dozen holes in the walls. The roof was

The house of Weng Fu was luxurious in the extreme.

made of straw, so thin that the rain demon, Yu Shih, laughed at it, and the stars peered in nightly. There was no *kang* (bed-stove), no table. Chairs were lacking. For furniture it had a heap of bean straw in a corner, a dozen bricks in another corner, a cupboard on a wall—thus was the house of Weng Fu furnished.

Weng Fu sat upon the earthen floor and bade Ah Tzu do likewise. "My son," said the beggar, "this is your future home—and excellent it is. This is your home—provided you prove worthy. But I warn you, I am hard to please. A son of mine must be as prompt as Ching Chi, as devoted as Wei Sheng, as brave as Meng Feu. Faithful and honest must my son be. You must ask no questions and do as I say. Otherwise, I shall beat you, and turn you out in the street. . . . Open the cupboard and bring me a bundle of straw." Ah Tzu obeyed. His new father continued: "Braid this straw into a pair of sandals. Work swiftly and have them finished by the time I return. And give me what money you have so that I may purchase food." Ah Tzu turned over his tiny bag of money. Then his fingers worked nimbly, braiding the straw.

Weng Fu returned in a very few minutes. His face was purple. His voice pitched high. "What? *Ya shu* [idle rascal]. Are you not finished? Well, you shall get no dinner till you complete the sandals." With that he put down a silver tray and began to eat. On the tray was roast duck. There were celery and tea-soaked eggs and rice and bean sprouts and brine-aged cabbage and almonds and garlic and many another dish of equal goodness. Weng Fu's teeth clicked busily. Every few seconds he grunted his satisfaction. Ah Tzu braided straw.

The silver tray was emptied long before Ah Tzu completed his task. Finally, "Here, my father, are the sandals, and I hope they will be to your liking," Weng Fu gazed. "They are not very well braided. But perhaps in time you will learn. Reach in the cupboard and get a bean cake for your dinner." Ah Tzu searched in the cupboard and found a small, hard, dry bean cake. "Here, give me half of it," ordered the queer father. "I am still hungry." The old fellow took at least three-fourths of the cake—all but a portion that had been nibbled by mice. Then he put on his new sandals, took up the tray, and departed. "Do not go out," he admonished Ah Tzu. "Stay here and guard the house against thieves." The door closed behind him. Just what a thief could have desired in that house would be hard to decide. Nevertheless, Ah Tzu stayed close at home, that night and the following day and the night that came after.

During the second night three men came to the door and tried to gain entrance, saying that they must have gold. Ah Tzu fanned about him so earnestly with a cudgel that all three were piled in a heap on the threshold. They went away limping and howling, one holding his hands to his pate, as if troubled with *nao tai teng* (as if troubled with head aching badly).

The next day saw Weng Fu's return. He asked Ah Tzu many questions, and Ah Tzu answered them. But the boy showed no inquisitiveness about the large bandage round Weng Fu's head, nor did he ask questions about Weng's bundle. The beggar finally opened his bundle and from it took food. He shared the food with his son—and this time he himself ate little. This time Ah Tzu had sufficient.

When the meal was finished, the beggar again opened his bundle and disclosed garments such as very young babies wear. "Put on these garments, my son. They will make you look many years younger. And I, seeing my son so young, will feel the years drop from my shoulders and be again in the prime of my manhood—at least ten years younger." Ah Tzu did as he was told. *"Cha, Tieh tieh"* (Certainly, Papa). On went the small garments. "Now, Ah Tzu, we'll go for a walk. Here is a calabash for you to rattle."

They went into the street. Ten steps, and a crowd gathered. Such jeering. Such laughter. "Ho. Ho. Ho. Here is old *back of the hands turned down* [a beggar] and his infant son. What a pretty baby! *Tieh tieh,* has your baby cut his teeth?" Ah Tzu rattled his calabash and tried hard to keep from blushing. Weng Fu sauntered on in utter unconcern. When they reached Seven Thieves Market, all shopkeepers boarded up their stalls, thinking a mob had come to plunder.

At home once more, Weng Fu produced more food and told Ah Tzu to eat. Then he cupped his hand to his ear as if listening. "I thought I heard someone shout my name. There it is a second time." He dashed out. At the door a bag fell from his girdle. The bag flew open, and from it rolled rubies and pearls, to a value of at least ten bars of gold. Ah Tzu called to his father, but receiving no answer, he hastily gathered up the baubles and hid them.

Night came, but with it no father. When the moon had been set for an hour, a noise brought Ah Tzu to his feet. The thieves? Let them come. The boy was expecting some such visitation. He had a stouter club and a kettle of hot water in readiness. . . . There was little short of murder done in the Street of the Place Where the Cow Lost Her

Horn. Ah Tzu had eaten strengthening food that night. Though he wore the clothes of an infant, that is no sign that his arm was the arm of an infant. Such howling.

Old Weng Fu merely grunted when he received the bag of rubies and pearls. Counting them he said, "I thought there were fifty large pearls." And he gazed keenly at Ah Tzu. If he expected to see a guilty flush, he was disappointed. "I did not count them, my father. All that I found I put in the bag." The beggar grunted. "So—here is the missing one. . . . But perhaps there were fifty-one. Look outside the door. You may find another."

As Ah Tzu sifted the earth, his nostrils told him of a smoke. Even as he straightened up, Weng Fu rushed from the house. No need to yell "Fire." Flames were darting like dragons' tongues out of the thatch, out of the walls. The old beggar ran in a circle, screaming: "Now what shall I crack nuts on? What? What? Oh. Oh. Oh. Ah Tzu, my son, get me the brick that lies on the floor in the northeast corner. The brick. The brick." Ah Tzu thought it strange that his father should set such high value on a brick. But, strange or not strange, an order was an order—to be obeyed. Shielding his face with a sleeve, he entered the house. Wisps of burning straw fell upon him. Smoke seared his eyes. Smoke griped his throat, periling his life. Straight he went to the farthest corner. He stopped. A quick dash. He was safe, beyond the door. Ah Tzu's task had been accomplished. He handed to his father a brick . . . a worthless yellow brick . . . a chipped and fissured brick. For that he had been made to risk his life.

Weng Fu spoke no word of praise. He did not so much as look at Ah Tzu. Only a close observer could have noticed that his lips quivered ever so slightly. Finally he said: "I have one more errand for you, my son; then you may rest. See—I have lost the string that bound my queue. Go you to the Emperor and ask His Majesty for an old ribbon. Tell the Emperor you wish to borrow a queue ribbon for Weng Fu, the beggar."

Sadly troubled, Ah Tzu hastened toward the palace. He had every reason for thinking that his impudent request would gain him, not a ribbon for Weng Fu, but a rope for his own neck . . . and death for Weng Fu.

It was the hour when Shang Tien Hao, the Emperor, sat in public audience. Any citizen might approach the throne. The aspen leaves never tremble so violently as Ah Tzu trembled, kneeling before his Monarch. With much stammering, he

His forehead was tight-pressed to the floor.

stated the business that brought him. All the time his forehead was tight-pressed to the floor.

Strangely enough, the Emperor made no beckon to the executioner. Instead, he smiled and said: "No, my son, I shan't give you a ribbon for old Weng Fu. He no longer exists. However, I shall give you ribbons aplenty and fine clothing for your own wear. You must learn that I, being without heir, dressed as a beggar, wandered the streets to find me a son as brave as Meng, as pure as Pao Shu, and as devoted as Wei. Such I found in you. No longer are you Ah Tzu, the orphan. Henceforth you are Lieh Shih—hero—and beloved son of Shang Tien Hao, the Emperor.''

Four Generals

Prince Chang petitioned his father, the King: "my honored parent, give me permission to make a journey throughout the kingdom. I would learn how the people live, and note wherein they are contented and discontented. Thus I shall be prepared against the time when I ascend the throne." The King nodded approval. "Your plan is good, my son. I shall imediately order that new gold tires be put upon the royal carriage, and summon ten troops of cavalry to guard you." But the prince would not listen to such arrangements. "Oh, no, sire, I mean to go alone and in disguise. Instead of the carriage, a stick will serve for my vehicle.

Instead of the troops, that selfsame stick will guard me."

Whereat, the King was greatly troubled, and the prince was put to much argument before he won his point. "Then do as you wish, my only and much beloved son," said the King, grudgingly. "But it behooves you to observe extreme care. Disorder is rife in all the provinces. Go, and may your stick be as strong as the magic mace of Sun How Erh."

"Farewell, my royal father."

"Farewell, my noble son."

Now, it must be remembered that Prince Chang was no graybeard. In years he was nearing thirteen. Is it, after all, such a great wonder that homesickness caused his heels to drag, and his eyes to need the kerchief? He had walked all of twenty li. That, he began to imagine, was journey enough for the present. To the edge of Hu Pei Forest he continued. At the edge of the forest he stopped. The woodland was so dark . . . so dark. The wolves howled "Oo-o-o-o-o-wh." (We starve.) And such a futile little stick with which to enter the forest of Hu Pei. "Oo-o-o-o-o-wh. What wolves . . .

The prince had turned his face toward home when a merry voice hailed him. "Ho. Brother, I'm glad you are come. Tell me if my fiddle be in tune." A comical fellow hopped down from a stump and chinned his fiddle while Prince Chang stared.

"Eek. Eek. Eeek." "How does it sound, little Brother?" "I dare say it—" But the fiddler was not waiting for an answer. His bow arm fell to sawing while his legs and voice joined in the tune —"A beggar asked the King to dine." And that's a foolish song. Prince Chang thought he had never before heard or seen anything so funny by half. The more he laughed, the greater his need for laughter. Such a comical beggar, and how he could play and sing!

From one end of Hu Pei Forest to the other, Prince Chang laughed while the beggar capered and fiddled. No wolves at all appeared. Homesickness was a thing of the past—forgotten. "Let me give you a copper cash, merry stranger," said Chang, when they came to a Y of the road. "Not now," said he of the fiddle and bow. "I judge you are poorer than I." "Indeed?" laughed the prince. "When I am King [he forgot himself there], I shall reward you handsomely." "Ho. Ho," shrieked the beggar. "When you are King. When you are King, I'll accept a reward. Make me a general in your army." "It shall be done," said Chang. "What is your very nice name?" "My pitiful name is Tang —Tang the fiddler. Farewell, my little King, who rides a bamboo horse." So they parted, both merry.

Sad to relate, Prince Chang's merriment was to

be of brief duration. A band of robbers sprang up from the roadside and surrounded him, pummeling him without mercy—all striking at one time. They took his stick and his clothing and the little bag of coins that hung from his neck. They left him in the road for dead. A sorry ending, that, to his journey . . .

Shortly, another traveler chanced by, and he was a man of warm heart. He revived Prince Chang and took him on his shoulder, carrying him to a village. There he set out food and clothing and bade the prince ask for what more he desired. Chang was deeply thankful. "How can I ever repay you?" "*Ya ya pei*" (Pish, tush), said the man. "It is nothing. What is a bit of food? And what is a gift of clothing? Besides, you must know that I am a tailor and will charge my next customer double. 'A tailor—a rogue,' says the proverb." "I do not believe it," exclaimed Chang, "and when I become King—" (There he forgot himself again.) "Ho. Ho. Ho." roared the tailor. "When you become King. Ho. Ho. When you are King, you may reward me. You may make me a general in your army." "It shall be done," declared Chang. "What is your honorable name?" "Wang is my miserable name. Wang the tailor. Farewell, and good luck be with you, my future King." So they parted, merrily enough—each laughing at the excellent jest.

Prince Chang continued his journey. For three days he saw no man of flesh and bone, nor came upon a dwelling. At the end of the third day he was weak and unsteady from hunger. His stick broke beneath his weight, and he lay beside the road, waiting for death to come. Instead of death, there came a shepherd with sheep and goats. The shepherd picked up Chang and saw that the boy was far spent. It was quite plain that hunger had used him evilly. Promptly the quick-witted fellow slung Chang on his shoulder and carried him off to a cave. Milk in bottles of leather hung on the cavern walls. Also, there were cheeses. Chang was made to drink of the milk—a little at first—only enough to moisten his throat. With the return of strength, he drank greedily, completely emptying a goatskin. And the emptier the bottle grew, the more he thanked the shepherd. "You have done me a great service," said Chang. "If I had money I—" "*Ya ya pei*" (Pish, tush), said the shepherd. "It is nothing. I fed you with no thought of reward." "Nevertheless," declared Chang, "when I am made King I—" The shepherd was like to strain his throat with guffawing. "Ho. Ho. Ho. When you are made King. What a merry chap you seem to be! Very well, when you are King you may reward me. Make me a general in your army. Ho. Ho. Ho.'' ''I shall. I shall.'' The prince was emphatic. ''What is your honorable name?'' ''My paltry name? Most folk call me Mang—Mang the shepherd. And here, you must carry some food with you, for the nearest house is thirty li distant. Take this cheese—and may good luck be your companion, my King of the wandering road.''

Burdened as he was, Prince Chang made slow work of getting over the mountain. He had begun to think seriously of dropping the cheese when a troop of soldiers clattered up the road behind him. ''How fortunate!'' said Chang. ''Here are my father's soldiers. They will take me on their horses to the next village.'' But the soldiers halted with a ''Who are you, and what brings you here?'' queried most fiercely and with scowls. The prince stammered that he was sometimes called Chun—a most unfortunate invention, for Chun was the name of a local bandit. The soldiers' frowns turned to pleased smiles (there was a reward offered), and the captain said: ''So you are Chun, and you have just robbed some poor person of a new suit and a cheese. Off with his head, my braves.'' Chang now saw that he was indeed in a tangle. A bold face seemed the only escape. He put

on a stern look, saying: "How dare you execute
men without a trial? Do you not know that I am
Prince Chang, son of your noble King?" The captain bowed in mock humility. "Your Highness
seems large for such a tender age. I happen to
know that King Yen Chi's eldest son is only two
years old. Let your swords drink, men."

The terrible truth was made plain to Chang. He
had wandered across the border of his father's
kingdom. He was in a neighboring and hostile
country. . . .

The swords were lifted to strike, when—swish—
came an arrow. After it, quickly, another, and
another. Each found its mark. For each arrow a
soldier crumpled. The others dug heels in their
horses, galloping pell-mell for their lives.

A stalwart youth stepped out from a pine. "You
had better go quickly," he said to Chang. "The
border of our own country lies a full mile back."
"I thank you with all my heart," declared Prince
Chang, "and shall reward you fittingly when—"
"When you are King?" finished the other. "I
heard what you said to the soldiers, and wondered
at your daring. Very well. Make me a general when
you become King, and that will be ample reward."
"It shall be done," vowed the prince. "What brave
name do you bear?" "Name? Oh, you may call me

Lang. Lang the very indifferent archer. And now you must go, for more soldiers will come, and my arrows are few."

Prince Chang was not long returned from his journey when the King passed away in an illness. Immediately the crown was placed on Chang's brow, and all the people burned much incense of *la ka* wood, crying, "Hail!" And almost with their next breath they shouted *"Kou chou!"* (The enemy!) An enemy was marching upon Ku Hsueh. The new King had barely seated himself upon the heighty throne before he found it necessary to see about raising an army. There were two great troubles with the old army. It was dwarfish small, and it boasted more generals than bowmen. Of course, the generals never fought. They did nothing but plan—usually what they'd have for dinner, and which sword they'd wear to the King's next reception. Yet, King Chang added more generals to the army.

The first complaint raised against King Chang by his people was that he had added four more generals to the army. His new generals were named Tang, Wang, Mang, and Lang—though doubtless such information is hardly necessary. They were old friends of the King. The four arrived at the capital in time to see a huge army of

The King and his generals gazed across the river.

hostiles encamp on the far side of the river that bordered the city. By great good fortune, the river was past fording, so holding the enemy in check. The King and his generals gazed across the river. Said he: "It is easily seen that the enemy has twenty men for every one we muster. What are your plans?" Of all his generals, only Wang seemed to have so much as the shadow of a plan. Wang said, "Give me all the tailors in the city, and all the cloth stored in the royal godowns." "Take them," said King Chang. "If you don't, the enemy will."

Throughout the night General Wang and his tailors slaved with needle and thread. The click of thimbles made a continuous humming sound. The hostiles on the farther shore heard, and wondered what strange warlike engines King Chang might be preparing.

With day's coming, Chang moved all his troops —he had only a thousand. The thousand men marched in parade along the river's brim. Their uniforms were old and dowdy. The words, "We are brave," that adorned their tattered jackets seemed a poor and weak boast. They were ragamuffins. They marched as if weary. The enemy jeered.

But, lo. The first thousand had no sooner disappeared than another thousand circled past the river—stepping smartly, smartly uniformed in cloth of gold, the words "Very brave" embroidered upon their fronts. The enemy was not so quick to jeer.

Following the second thousand came a thousand men in trig red uniforms. Upon their breasts were broidered the words "Extremely brave." They stepped it briskly, shouting dares across the river. The enemy replied with very little heart.

Another thousand followed. Jade-green uniforms clothed them. Rumbledumblededum sang their drums, and their steps kept perfect time. Upon their breasts were the words "Still braver," and upon their lips great threats. The enemy said little.

Now came men in crow's-wing black. Upon their breasts were the words "Braver by far." Their taunts were hard to bear. Yet, the enemy remained silent.

A thousand men in pink, the same number in blue. Came white-clad men and orange-clad men. Violet uniforms replaced uniforms of brown. . . . The enemy thought it hardly fair. King Chang, evidently, had a million soldiers. . . . How could they fight against a million? The tents came down, and the enemy vanished.

General Wang continued to sew until the last

hostile disappeared. He and his tailors were terribly tired. But the thousand soldiers were even more tired. All day long they had marched and changed uniforms, then marched again. They had changed from red to green, to black, to every color in the spectrum. They were color blind and weary. But King Chang married much, and blessed the day that had sent him General Wang, the tailor.

In a month or so King Chang's happiness turned to gloom. The enemy had learned of Wang's clever trick, and resolved to march again. The army of Chang was scarcely larger than before. To come off victorious each man would have to whip a dozen of the enemy. There was no time to increase the royal army. And the enemy lay on the other side of Ku Hsueh River, waiting for the waters to lower.

King Chang rode with his generals to the river. Said he: "There lies the enemy. The depth of the river lessens with each minute. Who has a plan?" Some of the generals stroked their beards. Others twisted their mustachios. All wrinkled their brows. Not one of them parted his lips. "Come. Come, my doughty generals. Have you no plan? General Tang?" Tang bowed his head the three times required by law and courtesy. "Sire, with your permission, I have a small scheme that may serve."

"Chen hao [Very good] ; spare no expense. Draw on the treasury for whatever you may desire—silk, tailors, fans, or false faces—anything except more soldiers, for soldiers we have not." "Then, please, Your Majesty," said Tang, "may I ask you to sign an order on the treasury for one ounce of pine resin?" Then the King thought Tang jesting. His first impulse was to strike off his head. Instead of doing so, however, he signed the order for two cents' worth of resin.

At night General Tang sat upon a crag that towered above the river. He fondled his precious violin. A little breeze sprang up at his back. Tang the general was no more, but Tang the musician lived and thrilled. Bow swept strings with a magic sweetly sad. The breeze caught up the melody. The river was its sounding board. The soldiers on the farther shore turned in their blankets to listen. Than home there is no spot dearer—and the violin sang of home. More and more sad came the music. The musician wept. Across the river ten thousand eyes grew moist. The soldiers wept and were unashamed. Why had they left their warm hearthstones—to die in an alien land? Fierce resolve faded, and a longing took its stead, a longing for home and the loved ones it sheltered.

Morning saw the hostile camp deserted. Soldier

More and more sad came the music.

after soldier had stolen away in the darkness, thinking only of home. Not one remained to threaten Ku Hsueh City.

King Chang assembled his generals, and spoke high praise of Tang. Then he discussed the need of preparation for the future. He knew very well that the enemy would return. "Have any of you, my trusty generals, a plan for humbling the enemy in his next invasion?" General Mang, the former shepherd, voiced a plan. "I would suggest that all

horses be replaced by lean sheep of the mountain.''
General Lang, the archer, said, ''I would suggest
that all cases at law be settled by trial with bow
and arrow.'' ''So be it,'' said the King. ''I grant
both requests.''

The enemy soon marched upon Ku Hsueh in
greater numbers than before. Grasshoppers in the
August fields were never thicker. It was plain that
only a miracle could save the city. All eyes were
turned to General Mang, turned beseechingly, and
rather doubtfully. Could a mountain shepherd
save Ku Hsueh?

That night the question was answered. Mang
herded his sheep in a tremendous body toward the
enemy camp. At the proper moment he raised a
great din and startled the animals into flight.
Through the camp of the enemy they rushed, and
instantly the camp was confusion. The soldiers had
fared none too well on their march. They were
hungry. And here was good food to be had for the
catching. Away went sheep. Away went soldiers.
Thoroughly frightened, the lean-limbed sheep sped
their fastest. Thoroughly desirous, the hungry soldiers followed at their fastest.

While the camp was empty, Mang and a score of
daring men darted from tent to tent. In their
hands were torches. Behind them rose a flare of

ever-spreading flame. "To roast their meat when they catch it," said Mang. The wind was a helpful friend, scattering brands with a will. The destruction was soon finished. What had been a white encampment became a red and rolling flame. The tents were burned, and the spears and the bows. Nothing was spared. A thoroughly discomfited enemy stole away from Ku Hsueh that night.

So far, General Lang had done nothing of a warlike nature—nothing at all—unless stepping upon the toes of a citizen be considered warlike. Lang had done that. Naturally, the citizen was incensed. He wished to see justice done, and went to a court of law. The judge said: "Take this bow and shoot five arrows in yonder target. He who shoots best has the right on his side." The young citizen shot first, and his marksmanship was poor, to say the least. Whereupon, Lang drew the bow. Oddly enough, his aim was no better than that of the citizen. With that the judge declared the suit undecided and set a future date for its retrial. General Lang left court well pleased. The young citizen went home to spend many hours in practice with bow and arrow.

Thereafter the courts were flooded with lawsuits. From morn till night the bowstrings twanged. It appeared that all the men of Ku

Hsueh had grievances to be settled. And they who were wise spent much time in archery practice ere they went to court. Many became quite expert with the bow and arrow. . . .

King Chang impressed all of them into his army. At last he had a large force, a force that would give pause to any foe. Long the King waited for his enemy's return. But he waited in vain. Spies had watched the men of Ku Hsueh at practice with the bow. They sent messages that Ku Hsueh was prepared. So the country was troubled no more by alarms of hostile armies.

Thus, without loss of a man, was the kingdom saved for Chang, by Wang, Tang, Mang, and Lang —a thousand years ago all this, but very learned men still dispute as to which was the greatest, Lang, Mang, Tang, or Wang—which of the four generals.

The Rain King's Daughter

The people of Shen Su were starving. A famine blighted all the land. Rice swamps yielded only empty husks. The millet fields were barren. The *ti tan* patches, for all their blossoms, produced no earth eggs—no potatoes. The *chu* groves gave no tender stalks. . . . And the people starved.

Every astrologer and wise man in the kingdom was summoned to King Ta Lang's palace. "Tell us, wise men, why we starve. Why is food denied us?" Thus the King questioned the graybeards, and they, the learned, consulted their charts and sand trays and crystal globes. One said: "The Shen of Falling Water, Yu Shih, is angry. We have burned no incense to him within a year." "It is a rat. A rat is eating our food," said another. The others, for the most part, echoed approval. "Yes," said they, "it is a rat."

"A rat ? Where is the rat ?"

"There, the mountain. The mountain we have called Che Chou."

King Ta Lang gazed in a line with their pointed fingers. At first, he saw merely a mountain. A longer look disclosed that the mountain was shaped like a crouching rat. "Trap the rat, and Shen Su will once more abound with food," declared the wise men.

"Yes, we must kill the rat," said King Ta Lang. "Ho, you carpenters, construct a giant *mu mao* [wooden cat] in the path of this terrible rat."

A huge wooden rattrap was built at the end of the mountain. Yet, the famine continued. Food became more and more scarce. The wise men announced that the trap was not properly built. The rat would not enter. They advised that a spear be thrust through his heart. Forthwith, King Ta Lang ordered that a great spear be driven through the heart of the mountain. A spear would surely kill the rat. But not so. Beneath the earth of the mountainside was flint-iron-hard flint. A thousand soldiers thrusting could not drive the spear deeper than its point.

While the soldiers struggled vainly to pierce the flinty core, a little blaze leaped from dry pine needles. Their iron had brought sparks from the stone. The little blaze leaped from the needles to a bush, and from the bush to a tree. Then it was a large blaze. Soon a whole acre of mountainside blazed fiercely. The soldiers ran away. At first, they were badly frightened, thinking the King would be angry. But the King said: "That is splendid. Why didn't my wise men think of it? The rat will be grandly singed. Ho. Ho. Ho. He will be burned to his death."

There was good reason for thinking as King Ta Lang thought. The fire spread up and down till the whole mountain blazed. The mountain was a solid wall of flame, and above it spread a vast sea of smoke. Only an extremely hardy rat could live through such intense heat and suffocating fumes.

Now, there is no telling why the heavens opened. Perhaps the heat of blazing Mount Che Chou burned a hole in the sky. Perhaps the Rain Shen, Yu Shih, imagined the people had burned incense to his honor. However that may be, it is certain that the heavens *did* open. Upon burning Mount Che Chou, the rain leaped down in cataracts, and the lightning played continuously. Over the plains of Shen Su also the waters fell, but there the rain was gentle, though persistent.

For seven days the skies dripped. Then the grass was as green as jade. The cattle filled their so-loose coats. Quick-growing vegetables sprang up in every garden. There was life. All the people of Shen Su said: "The rat has been singed by the fire. The rat has been drowned by the waters. His head has been cleft by the lightnings. Now he is dead and cannot steal our food." And that was their belief. "The rat is no more—therefore we have food and life."

While the rain still plashed on the roof tiles, new life came to the palace. A son was born to King Ta Lang. At that same hour a basket was found in the garden. In the basket was a tiny girl. No one had been seen to place the basket. Here was mystery. Again King Ta Lang summoned his soothsayers. He wished to learn what the coming years held in store for his son. Further, he wished to learn the past as well as the future of that chubby little girl so mysteriously cradled in his garden.

The wise men consulted book and glass and table. All in good time Ta Lang learned that his son must be named Tou Meng (Give Thanks) and that he would remain great as long as he remained thankful. The girl must be named Chai Mi (Enables Us to Live). Chai Mi was a daughter of the Rain King, Yu Shih, who had given her to become the wife of Tou Meng.

King Ta Lang was well pleased. Evidently the

At that same hour a basket was found in the garden.

rain monarch meant to be friendly. Prince Tou
Meng and the wee Princess Chai Mi were betrothed by royal decree. They played with the same
golden calabash. They drank from the same porcelain bowl. Each cried because of the other's terrible misfortunes—toes will get bumped and favorite
toys go astray, even in the royal nursery. Each
laughed when the other was gay. In short, they
played and laughed, and bickered and made up,
much like brothers and sisters the wide world over.

Quickly sped the years. The prince added inch after inch to his stature. The height of the princess increased in proportion. If she was not so tall, she seemed equally strong and daring. She played ball with the prince. She climbed trees and rode donkeys. She could place her arrow in the target's eye, and she could swim where few would venture. More, the princess could broider, and sew, and dance most gracefully—not in the depraved and shameless manner of today; she danced the olden dances. And Chai Mi was a discreet maiden. She took good care not to excel Prince Tou Meng. If the prince's arrow struck the second ring, then her arrow came no inch closer to the mark. When swimming, the prince always won his races by the slightest margin. They were often in the water, those two. The river Lan cut its swift way through the palace grounds. Each summer day it felt the strokes of Chai Mi and Tou Meng.

In the river, Princess Chai Mi found a roll of parchment, written upon with characters she did not know. She took it to the King. Then there was excitement intense, with soldiers gathering from all directions. For the letter that the river had given to Chai Mi was a secret letter written by an enemy. It disclosed that the enemy was marching on Shen Su. "Here," said the wise men, "is fresh proof that the King of Rains is our friend. He has disclosed our terrible enemy's perfidy."

The drums sounded a continuous call as King Ta Lang mustered his army. Prince Meng buckled on a sword that dragged the earth. But Chai Mi— sewed. "You cannot go, Thousand Pieces of Gold," they told her. "You have done more than well in discovering the danger, but you cannot fight." So Chai Mi sat beside the river, and sewed and wept, while the sound of drums grew fainter and fainter.

Then there was silence. Shen Su City was peopled only by women. Not only the women wept, but the skies. For three days it rained without ceasing, and the river Lan became fat with much

So Chai Mi sat beside the river, and sewed and wept.

water, too large for its bed. It rose above its banks, and there was no crossing. Its voice was loud, threatening—the voice of Yu Shih, Master of Waters, shouting defiance.

Down to the river by cover of night hurried a silent army. At the water's edge it halted. No mortal man could dare that snarling current, and live. No soldier with spear and shield could hope to swim such a maddened torrent. And boats there were none—Yu Shih had torn them from their ropes, had carried them down to the sea. The army must wait. Let it rest in the mud, and await Yu Shih's permission to cross.

When day came, the women of Shen Su City beheld an immense army on the river's far side. It was the hostile army that King Ta Lang had marched to intercept. Beyond a doubt, the King had taken a wrong road. The enemy had eluded him, slipped past him unseen. Only Lan River in flood prevented the hostiles from entering Shen Su. And the river could sink as suddenly as it rose.

Now, when King Ta Lang marched away, he went in haste, and lightly burdened. All heavy armor was left behind, all heavy spears and shields. This was known to the Princess Chai Mi. She thought of the empty armor, thought of the long-shafted spears. With men to hold them, those

spears could save the city. But there were no men
—only a few who were unable to march.

However, there were women, many of them
badly frightened, some who were calm and un-
afraid. Chai Mi quickly made known her plan.
Then Shen Su City awoke from its silence. Ham-
mers clashed on armor, making the rivets secure.

In the enemy camp appeared a man who knew
no fear of the river. He swam the raging Ho Lan
and drew himself up on the other shore. Girdling
his waist was a rope. The rope was soon tied to a
willow stump. After that, the passage was much
easier. One at a time, bearing only their bows, the
enemy crossed. Their chieftain, to set an example,
was among the first. Thus, by aid of the rope, a
number of the enemy swarmed over. They felt
perfectly safe from attack. Their information was
that Ta Lang had taken all his soldiers with him.
Shen Su would be an easy prey. Five hundred men
should be sufficient. And that many had crossed the
river.

From Shen Su City marched a thousand braves,
clad in glistening armor, bearing those tremendously long spears called *chang chiang*. Of course,
they wore hideous false faces. That was the custom
of all Eastern soldiers. Behind the spear bearers
marched a thousand archers. The wall of Shen Su

Of course, they wore hideous false faces.

suddenly bristled with spears, a thousand more. The enemy could not retreat. There was the river to hinder. To advance seemed utter folly. What effect could little arrows have on weighty armor? And how could five hundred prevail against six times and more their number? To surrender seemed the only course, and that is what they did. But it was grievous hard. Their leader was of royal blood. No worse disgrace could have been his lot.

Those on the shore beyond were made to cast their weapons in the river. With their royal leader a prisoner, they dared not disobey, for fear he would be slain. Their captors looked quite capable of such action. The crestfallen enemy had no faintest dream that those captors were . . . girls . . . led by Chai Mi. How could they know? The deceit was well concealed. An ancient little tailor did the talking, and he, proud of his chance to swagger, talked with a terrible voice—violently threatening. But Chai Mi, resplendent in the King's golden armor, told him what to say. And the other maids clashed their spears upon the river stones, as if angry at being deprived of living targets.

King Ta Lang in his swan-shaped sampan was crossing Lan River when he heard of Chai Mi's stirring deed. He could scarce believe his ears. The couriers vowed that they spoke no exaggeration. Convinced at last, the King said: "Then Chai Mi has done us a great service. She shall receive honors without stint." But the King's chief general was more than jealous because Chai Mi had succeeded where he had failed. This general said, "Has Your Majesty forgotten the law?"

"What law?" asked King Ta Lang.

"The law made by your illustrious ancestor Liu Ti. The law of Liu Ti says that no woman may put on the habiliments of a King. Death is the penalty for so doing. The maiden put on Your Majesty's armor."

The King heard with grief. He said: "That is truth. There is such a law, and laws, good or bad, must be enforced. By the law of my noble ancestor, the maiden Chai Mi must lose her head by the sword."

And the jealous general said, "Here is a death warrant for your signature."

Now, whether the King would really have beheaded Chai Mi, no man can say. His boat suddenly disappeared beneath the waters, and was seen no more. The wise men said that he had excited the wrath of Yu Shih, Master of Waters, and father of the maiden. That may, or may not, be true. Again, no man can say.

But this can be said, without fear of dispute. King Meng and his Queen ruled over Shen Su for many a year, and there was neither flood nor famine—only a great tranquillity.

Many Wives

This is the story that Kung Lin tells, hour after hour, in the peaceful shade of Bell That Rings Often Temple. The people have relish for Kung Lin's favorite story, and give him much money. The tattered old fellow sometimes receives as much as five cents—in a single day. So outrageously fortunate is Kung Lin, the teller of tales. He does no work of any kind whatsoever, merely sits in the shade, and talks, and hears the tinkle of coins in his bowl, and hears the people saying: "It is well told, Kung Lin. Here is some money—and I hope you find it as good as your story." Not all makers of yarns find such sympathetic hearers.

As the story is given by Kung Lin, there once lived a maiden named Radiant Blossom, and she was still more lovely than the loveliest maiden.

The face of Radiant Blossom was shaped like a seed of the melon. It was regularly oval, wide at the brow, small as to chin. The maiden's eyebrows were like a leaf of the willow. Her eyes resembled the heart of an apricot. Her lips in color made cherries seem pale. Her feet were three-inch golden lilies. And when she walked, she swayed as a poplar sways in summer zephyrs.

Furthermore, she was skilled in embroidery. Her fingers coaxed sweetest music from flute and lute. Her voice had its only rival in a fountain of the palace, where water plashes on tuneful silver keys. A brief description, this, but even so—where within the Province of Many Rivers, journeying by boat of two sails or three, could one look for a maiden to surpass Radiant Blossom, daughter of Ming Chi, red-button mandarin, and proud?

Hear now of the reigning Emperor, Wong Sing. That illustrious monarch was having a fine time in the ruling of his realm. He dined in heavy armor and slept with a saddle for pillow. It was war here, and battle there, and fighting in between. A dozen of his generals were in revolt. No sooner was a rebellion put down than two new ones, and worse, took its place. And there was trouble elsewhere— outside the empire. Fierce Barbarians, led and inspired by their haughty chieftain, Wolf Heart, grew every day more impudent and threatening. Wolf Heart openly boasted that with the coming of pleasant weather he intended to leap his horse over the Great Wall. Is it any wonder that Wong Sing's noble beard soon took on a hue like that of the lime boys splash on fences?

But Wong Sing was no weakling monarch, to lose his crown and his head, saying: "It was willed by the Fates. What else could I do?" He called in a fearless old councilor known as Ching Who Speaks Only Enough. Said the Emperor: "Good Ching, although you are ever up to your ears in a book, perhaps you have heard of my numerous troubles —a new one, I think, every day. What, wise Ching, is the cure?"

Ching Who Speaks Only Enough replied, "Marriage."

The Emperor raised his eyebrows. "Marriage?" He could hardly believe it. "Marriage to put down rebellion?" A pause. "Huh."

Ching repeated, and a trifle louder, "Marriage."

Still the Emperor doubted. "What? Marriage? Will marriage cause Wolf Heart to sheathe his sword? Marriage to tame the Barbarian? It is foolishness. But surely I misunderstand your words."

But indeed he did not. And there was only one

word. "Marriage." That was all the advice most mighty Wong Sing could get from word-stingy old Ching Who Speaks Only Enough.

However, is not enough always enough? Is not a word to the wise like melon seeds planted in fertile ground? A little study soon convinced the puissant Wong Sing that old Ching had given good advice. Immediately he acted upon it. He wrote to every mandarin of any consequence within the bounds of his empire. The letters are too long to quote, but the sum of them was this: "I, Wong Sing, Ruler of the Earth, and the Moon, and three-fourths of the Sun, will consider it a favor to receive your beauteous Thousand-Pieces-of-Gold in marriage."

Every mandarin replied by sending to the palace a daughter. No magic could have stopped the rebellions quicker. Revolt was at an end. Could a rebel leader, no matter how determined, continue to rebel when all his colonels and majors and half his captains were fathers-in-law to the Emperor? It was impossible. The fighting was over in a twinkling. Marriage had done it.

For months came damsels to the royal palace. And what damsels they were! Short and tall, lean and stout, young and old, perfect beauties and perfectly horribles, they came and came and came. It is hard to number them with exact figures. Some histories say that five thousand maids came to Wong Sing, his wives to be. Others vow to ten thousand. But why quarrel over a difference of a few thousand wives? The point is that they were numerous. Wong Sing was out of pocket several tons of gold for the construction of a wing to the palace for housing them all. Probably fifteen thousand was the correct figure.

Surely, the worst guesser in the world would in time conclude that the beautiful Radiant Blossom was among the Emperor Wong's twenty thousand wives. Of a certainty she was. Radiant Blossom came to the palace in the month of Ripening Apricots. It was midwinter before she so much as glimpsed her lord and master, the Emperor. And then she saw him only for a moment, at a distance.

For Wong Sing was very like the old man—or was it a woman—who lived in a sandal—or whatever it was. He had so many wives he scarce knew what to do. And is it any wonder? Imagine a staid and settled old bachelor's sudden gain of five or thirty thousand—or more—wives. Poor Wong admitted a few dozen of them to a reception, and in less time than it takes to tell, all the palace physicians were busily binding ice to his fevered brow. They thought his mind was shattered.

After that experience the Emperor was more

careful. He summoned the court artist, one Loh Yang, and said: "Loh Yang, I desire you to paint truthful portraits of all my wives. When the paintings are finished, bring them to me, that I may decide which maid is most beautiful. Her I shall take as my really truly bride."

Now, Loh Yang was an artist of ability, and no denying. But he was a scamp and a half. The first portrait he painted was that of Ying Ning, a monstrous ugly maiden. But Ying Ning was quite rich —and liberal. She gladdened Loh Yang's dishonest palm with gold. And he portrayed her as marvelously beautiful. Of all Loh Yang's paintings, the portrait of Ying Ning is most sightly. Yet she was the very ugliest of Wong Sing's many wives.

By and by it came Radiant Blossom's turn to sit for a portrait. Loh Yang suggested that for a moderate weight of gold—say ten pounds—he could make his brush fairly outdo itself. Radiant Blossom refused, with indignation. "Bribe you? To paint me as I am not? Never." Loh Yang begged for pardon. He seemed extremely penitent. He vowed that he would do his best work. But when the portrait was finished, it was enough to frighten the blind. The shameless rascal had made of lovely Radiant Blossom a gruesome crone, a witch, a slattern. Upon beholding it, the Emperor

*The first portrait he painted was that of Ying Ning, a
monstrous ugly maiden.*

covered his eyes with a sleeve. "Horrors. Horror of horrors. Remove it instantly. Go. Go. Take it away. Such repulsive ugliness."

It is a mere waste of words to add that Radiant Blossom was not chosen to be Wong Sing's own, really truly, and well-beloved bride.

The braggart Barbarian chief failed of his promise to leap over the Great Wall. Knowing that Wong Sing's armies were united and staunch, Wolf Heart boasted no more, and his impudence was hushed. He thought it just as well to keep the peace. And when Wong Sing doubled-doubled his armies, the Barbarian sent thick letters in which every line told of his long-felt love and respect for the Emperor. He had the audacity to ask Wong for a wife—from the Imperial Palace. Of course, that was purest impudence, in a way, though Wolf Heart probably thought that he was being extremely nice.

The Emperor read in amaze. For a moment it seemed that his face would burst into flame, so red it got. Then he smiled. "A wife? To be sure I will send him a wife. Chancellor, what is the name of that maiden whose picture is so terrible? Radiant Blossom? Bid Radiant Blossom prepare for a long journey. I am sending her to the Barbarian to be his wife. Ho. Ho. Ho. What a jest! I should like to hear Wolf Heart's rage when he views her. Ugh. I shudder when I think of that horrible crone.''

The maiden Radiant Blossom heard her sentence without the faintest stir of emotion. There came no pallor to her cheeks. No tremble moved her lips. Seemingly, it mattered not at all to her. And while the other maidens wept for her fate, she smiled and brushed the string of her lute, humming, ''Butterfly that pleasured yesteryear.''

A few hours more and Radiant Blossom was seated in a gilt and lacquered sedan chair, borne by poles on the shoulders of royal slaves traveling in haste toward the setting sun. Poor Radiant Blossom, hastening into exile, pressing toward her doom, to become the bride of a vandal. Not dew, but tears from the darkness descended. The nightingale's song was a sobbing of pity. The very trees that lined the road soughed deep despair. To the river. To the river, where on the farther shore waited Wolf Heart, the slaves hurried through the night.

His Majesty, Wong Sing, dressed him in rough clothing, and by another highway made even greater speed to the river. He wished to be near when the Barbarian greeted his bride. He wished to gloat over Wolf Heart's surprise and furious resentment. Expecting a youthful and lotus-like maiden, how the Barbarian would rave to behold a withered hag! His Majesty, the Emperor, expected to receive more than a little pleasure to pay him for the adventure.

The light sedan that bore Radiant Blossom sped down to the river. A flower-hung sampan was waiting. The slaves put down their burden. Oars splashed. The shore sprang back. The swifting current was deep beneath. . . .

Did the curtains of the gilt sedan flutter aside?

Was it a spirit that glided so quickly from the royal sedan?

A slave shouted warning. His cry was taken up by the others. The oars stopped short in stroke. Torches flared. The boat listed heavily on its side as men swarmed to the railing. They talked in frightened squeaks. "Where?" squeaked one, "There," from another. And "I see nothing." "She is gone." "Drowned." "The river took her to be his bride." "Drowned—and our necks will pay."

Wolf Heart uncovered his wrath in all its blackness. He spoke with such fury that Wong Sing became frightened, and offered to send another bride—a dozen brides. The Barbarian refused to accept brides. He demanded gold—much of it. Gold, he said, could not leap into the river. And even if it did leap from a boat, it would not necessarily be lost.

For that matter, a maiden may leap from a boat and not necessarily be lost. Radiant Blossom had passed her early days in the Province of Many Divers. Her home had been a river. She knew the waters as a friend.

Having leaped from the boat, Radiant Blossom permitted the river to hide her for long. Deeply she swam, and the clouded current was a veil. At last, when she knew that the torches were far behind, she arose. The night was another veil.

To the hut of a fisherman went Radiant Blossom. She received coarse clothing that made of her, in look, a different maiden. Thus clad, she journeyed to the home of her father.

Some time later a portrait was brought to His Majesty, the Emperor Wong Sing. The portrait was that of a beautiful maid. It bore no words. Wong Sing offered much gold to any person who could tell him the name of one so beautiful. The maiden would make him a superlative wife. He wished to find her. But he never did.

That Lazy Ah Fun

Chu Ping was a good man. He was clever and industrious, and wore his pigtail long. No one knows why he was cursed with such an indolent offspring as that lazy Ah Fun. Perhaps the vice was inherited, with a skip, from Grandfather Chu Ping Fu. They do say in Lao Ya Shen that Grandfather Chu Ping Fu was too lazy even to burn yellow paper on New Year's Eve, or to beat a copper pan in order to scare away the demons. But no matter about Chu Ping Fu. Let nothing more be said of him. Not Chu Ping Fu, but his graceless grandson is herein to be held up for scorn.

That lazy Ah Fun—for such everyone called him—was nothing if not a sluggard, and so he had been from the cradle. What a shameless creature he was—a snail— a lame snail at that. Dr. Chu Ping sent him with a bamboo tube of brick dust to the house of Chang Chi, where Mrs. Chang lay sick with a fever, and greatly in need of the medicine. And did Ah Fun hasten on his errand? No. A thousand times, no. He dawdled. He took his own, his very own time, that lazy Ah Fun. Poor Mrs. Chang, may she go to a good reward, was three days dead and in her paper coffin before Ah Fun finally arrived with the medicine that was meant to save her.

Now, that is but a single instance, and a sad one, of the way in which Ah Fun was wont to dilly and to dally. Here is another illustration. Dr. Chu Ping dispatched his son to the pasture land, there to find the cow and fetch her home for milking. Dr. Chu Ping knew the boy's habit, so he sent him when the sun was highest, at noon, in order that he might get the cow home before darkness came. But Ah Fun went nowhere near the pasture. He sat in the shade, playing the noisy game of "guess fingers" with a comrade in idleness. And when night came, he went to the yard of Low Moo, his next-door neighbor, and drove the Low cow into his own yard. It was so much easier than walking way down to the pasture land for his own cow.

Dr. Chu Ping had milked the cow, and the cow had kicked the bucket over before Low Moo came in tears, declaring that he had been greatly wronged and that Ah Fun should be whipped with a bamboo. The other neighbors gathered round, and without exception they said: "That lazy Ah Fun; he is no good. He should be beaten." But the doctor said that Ah Fun meant no harm—he was merely too tired to go to the pasture, and that someday—(here he thumped vigorously on the bucket, rum tum tum—one always makes a noise to scare the demons, when saying complimentary things)—someday Ah Fun would be a very famous man, and have a monument half a li in height, covered with much carving to tell his praise.

Then the neighbors said, "Humph," and the way they said it was with the corners of their mouths turned down, sneeringly. Clearly, they disbelieved. And one said, "There was never a hyena that didn't think his own son fairer than the King's child." The good doctor laughed heartily at that. He turned to Ah Fun and said (pounding on the bucket): "Ah Fun, treasure of my miserable heart, take you the bucket, and going to the well, fetch us home some water, for there is no milk, the terrible cow having kicked it over. Hence we can have only water with our Evening Rice. And be sure, my chiefest comfort"—rum dum, went the bucket—"to rinse the bucket thoroughly, twice at least."

So Ah Fun took the *shui tung* (the bucket), and

pretended he was going to the well. But the well was a li, a third of a mile distant. The ditch was only a few steps distant. That lazy Ah Fun stopped at the ditch and filled his *shui tung*. He came home with a bucket half full of green ditchwater. And in the water was an old shoe, a discarded shoe, a shoe that someone had thrown away as worn out and utterly useless. Nor had the bucket been rinsed.

But Dr. Chu Ping, instead of scolding Ah Fun, scolded the excellent people of Lao Ya Shen, saying: "This town is getting very very bad. One cannot walk decently and in peace from the well to one's house, but that some scamp must toss an old shoe in the water bucket." What a deluded man was that Dr. Chu Ping!

When the spring rains were at their heaviest, Dr. Chu Ping was called from this house to that house to visit the ailing. The rains caused much sickness, and the doctor was out at all hours, no matter how foul the weather. In consequence, he was more often wet than dry, and the wetness worked against his health. One night he came home dripping water from every thread of his garments, and his teeth were chattering, upper against lower. He crawled upon the *kang,* which is both stove and bed, saying, as well as he could: "Ah Fun, my blessing most cherished, build a fire under the

kang. Your so miserable old father has a chill that
no doubt will end his wholly useless existence.
Build a tremendous fire, Ah Fun, my precious
jewel. *Ai ya,* I am cold and ill.''

Ah Fun tore a few leaves of paper from a medicine book, and inserting them under the *kang,*
struck fire to them. Then he resumed his play.
After a while Dr. Chu Ping raised the quilt from
his head and hoarsely whispered, ''I—I—I am still
shivering, Ah—Ah Fun. M-m-more w-w-wood.''
Ah Fun looked about, but he saw no firewood. And
he was too lazy to go in search. However, the
doctor's gold-crested cane stood in a corner. Well,
why not? It was bamboo. It would burn. Into the
kang went the cane, and right pleasantly did it
crackle. But after a time Dr. Chu Ping again uncovered his head and begged weakly, ''M-m-more
w-w-wood, Ah—Ah Fun!'' Once more Ah Fun
looked round the room. There was positively no
firewood in sight. However . . . upon a shelf lay
half a hundred bamboo cylinders, tubes that contained medicines. In one bamboo was cuttlefish
bone. In another was *ko fen* (powdered oyster
shell). The doctor had used that on old Mrs. Fuh
Lung's rheumatism, with good effect, too. In a
third were salt and *chieh tzu.* A fourth held *chen pi*
and *shih hui* (orange peel and lime). The fifth

contained *chang nao* (camphor, and ashes) . . . all good medicines, and valuable indeed.

But . . . what did Ah Fun do? He chucked the first bamboo tube into the *kang,* and the tube crackled as the flames bit through. Presently, he cast in the second tube. Followed the third and fourth. Tube after tube, medicines and all, went into the *kang,* atop which lay Dr. Chu Ping.

Now, it so happened that the fiftieth tube contained *huo yao* (*the* medicine) and *huo yao* is made of sulfur, saltpeter, and charcoal—those three, the very three that combine to make gunpowder—as we call it—nothing less.

Dr. Chu Ping lay upon the *kang,* all atwitch with the chill that had worsted him. His son, Ah Fun, threw into the *kang* a large tube of *huo yao.* The fire crackled smartly, eating the tube. . . . Then . . . "BROOOOMP."

Oh, that terrible Ah Fun! He has blown up the bed-stove. To say nothing of his honorable father.

It was raining heavily, but just the same Mrs. Low Moo came out and upbraided the doctor unmercifully for coming down in, and utterly havocking, her patch of *huang ya tsai* (her tender, pretty cabbages). She told him her every thought upon that subject, with such words as *"Hun chang tung hsi"* (Stupid, blundering old thing you). But

"BROOOOMP."

Dr. Chu Ping merely gazed sheepishly at the destroyed cabbages, and at the hole in the room through which he had been blasted, and murmured, *"Kai tan"* (Ah, me, what a pity).

And again came the other neighbors, the very kind people who loved Dr. Chu Ping and wished to help him in his troubles. These well-wishing neighbors came and said: "Beyond a doubt, that boy is to blame. Honorable Doctor, why do you not break many stout bamboos upon the back of that boy— that lazy good-for-nothing Ah Fun? He will be the disgrace of, and the death of you yet." But Dr. Chu Ping rubbed his shoulder, and said: "What? Beat Ah Fun? Why, he is a good boy and a comfort. He just built me an excellent fire in the *kang.*"

Then the doctor limped into his house and awoke Ah Fun, asked him what had happened. Ah Fun, though he was bad—goodness knows, terribly bad —yet was truthful. Reluctantly, we must give him credit for that. He told of all that had happened: how he placed tube after tube in the *kang*—being unable to discover any firewood—and how the last tube had exploded, hurling his father through the roof.

Dr. Chu Ping wrinkled his brow till it was all hills and hollows. He pulled his long and neatly

braided hair in a highly meditative manner. He felt
first his right shoulder, then his left shoulder. He
rolled his eyes upward to the limit of their travel.
He gazed at the hole in the roof, where still flut-
tered a fragment of clothing on a jagged edge. He
rolled his eyes downward and scrutinized the
ruined *kang*. He felt of his two ears that still
reverberated with the enormous explosion. Then
he spoke. "My son," said he, "it strikes me that we
are on the verge of a great discovery. One of those
medicines—though gracious knows which one—
seems to be more than a medicine. It is good for
something else—though dear knows what. Perhaps
to grow wings, so that men may fly. It certainly
enabled me to fly. We must make more medicines,
and experiment."

The next day Dr. Chu Ping opened his book of
instructions for the compounding of medicines—a
book that he himself had written. Beginning at the
very beginning—which, of course, was on the last
page—good Dr. Chu studied the first formula.
"Red pepper, and alum, and toad claws," so he
read. The three ingredients were found and mixed
in the specified proportions. The mixture was
poured into a bamboo tube, and the tube was
placed in a fire. For an hour Dr. Chu Ping stirred
the fire and fanned it into furious blazing. Nothing

but much heat and much smoke resulted. There was no noise and no flying. Clearly, the combination of pepper, alum, and toad claws was quite worthless—except in the treatment of scarlet fever, for which it is intended. The doctor made a careful writing of the experiment and turned another page.

Next came oyster shell and ginseng. Worthless that, also. Shark fins and turmeric. Dr. Chu Ping marked that likewise as worthless. So the experimenting continued, day after day. It took a great deal of time. The doctor was a most thorough man, as well as brilliant. One couldn't find a more thorough or brilliant in all Kiang Su or Kiang Si or even in Kuang Si. Methodically he tried his medicines in the fire—by one and one he tried them— and thus he came to the mixture *huo yao,* which, to repeat is sulfur and saltpeter and charcoal, and which the Fan Kwei, or Foreign Devils, with their white faces call gunpowder. Dr. Chu Ping placed a long tube of *huo yao* in the fire. He leaned over it, fanning vigorously. For a moment the tube lay on the coals, sizzling and swelling, seeming to gather its breath for a supreme effort. . . . Zzzzzzz . . . Zeeeee . . . BROOOOMP.

And up went Dr. Chu Ping.

Now, it so chanced that a moment before the

explosion, old man Low Moo was milking his cow. A moment after the explosion, he was *not* milking his cow. He was running for dear life in a northerly direction. His cow was running for dear life in a southerly direction. And Dr. Chu Ping sprawled upon the flattened bucket and the smashed stool, where he had fallen.

The doctor came to in five minutes. Old Mr. Low Moo came back in half an hour. The cow has never since been seen. It is doubtful if she will ever return.

No sooner did Dr. Chu Ping revive than he hobbled into the house, where Ah Fun sat calmly playing with a *pan pu tao,* a little toy man who has round feet, and always regains an upright position, no matter how often he is knocked over. "What happened, my father?" asked Ah Fun. Dr. Chu Ping beamed upon him. "Ah Fun, my pearl, my jade, my orange tree, it is discovered. *Huo yao* is the great medicine. And it is good for scaring demons. Old man Low Moo, as everyone knows, is possessed of a demon—and he was frightened horribly. And his unkind cow, which is guided by at least four and twenty demons, has been frightened completely out of the country. There can be no doubt—*huo yao* is a frightener of demons. And you and I are the discoverers. Oh, my precious one, we

Dr. Chu Ping beamed upon him. "Ah Fun, my pearl, my jade, my orange tree, it is discovered."

shall be famous. A thousand thousand years from now men will still use *huo yao* to scare the demons."

And that was a very good prediction. *Huo yao* is still placed in tubes, little paper tubes, and the fuses are lighted, and "Sput, sput." The fire-crackers explode, and a thousand demons tremble and flee, reviling the names of Ah Fun and Dr. Chu Ping, who invented gunpowder.

The Moon Maiden

King Chan Ko was more than a Monarch. He was one of the best soothsayers in all the discovered world, having studied under no less a master than the famous Chai Lang. Even the most skeptical, then, will admit that Chan Ko as a geomancer must have stood far above the average. Chai Lang was particular in the selection of his pupils.

Once each week, at its beginning, His Majesty was accustomed to casting the signs, so that he might know what to expect. Thus, if rain was due on a Wednesday he was forewarned, and fore-umbrellaed. And if war was predicted for Friday, he was forearmed and ready to give two blows for one. He knew of the third flood a whole week before it happened, and, you may be sure, had a palatial boat provisioned and ready—laden with rice and musical instruments—a good three days before the waters came.

Rather unexpectedly, it became imperative for King Chan Ko to take horse on an urgent journey. Despite the call for great haste, he refused to make one step before casting the signs—though to do so made necessary an hour's labor. On his plane Chan Ko scribed the three circles with their bisecting lines. He drew the sun, moon, and stars in their relative places, gazed for a moment . . . and groaned, *"Ai yu,"* and *"Hai ya."*

Well might he groan. There was no error in the work. No other reading was possible. Upon the following night a dragon would swoop down from the moon and carry off the Princess Yun Chi. That was the reading, and there could be no doubting its truth. It may be imagined that gray hairs made quick appearance in the Monarch's beard. His journey was highly necessary. No postponement could be arranged. Yet, the Princess Yun Chi, his daughter, was well beloved, and not to be given up so long as sword had temper and javelin was sound of shaft. But—who was to wield sword, who to thrust javelin? Who indeed? Who if not the fourscore and ten valiant young princes of the realm, who even then deplored a dearth of daring deeds to be performed. No sooner the thought, than King Chan Ko summoned the princes into audience. Briefly he described the peril that threatened— told of the dragon's cunning, of his strength that increased with every blow, given or received. Not a pleasant picture King Chan Ko drew—at first. But when in conclusion he stated the reward, every prince in the chamber drew sword, and wished that the dragon might come forthwith. For, said Chan Ko, "If all of you together slay the *loong,* then if she so pleases, the princess may make her choice of you. But if any prince, unaided, slays the *loong,* then I say to you that such victorious prince and none other shall wed the Princess Yun Chi."

There was such a clanking of armor that the magpies clustering the palace roof made off on wing. There was such a testing of newly strung bows that the sky rained arrows for a whole day.

Prince Ting Tsun, as comely warrior youth as ever twirled sharp steel, took to himself a notion that his sword alone must blood the dragon. He can hardly be censured. Anyone is likely to be greedy when a royal princess is in danger, and her hand awaits an heroic defender. But Ting Tsun with his bravery mixed sagacity. To himself he reasoned thus: "Suppose I do succeed in killing the moon dragon? Will his infuriated brothers not come seeking vengeance? Without doubt they will. My only hope is to slay them all—now—and their ruler with them. Then the danger will be removed forever, and I can eat rice in comfort, without the need of a sword on the table. I must kill all of the moon *loongs.*"

With such an ambitious plan in mind, Prince Ting Tsun visited a sewing woman and had her make him a cloak precisely like that worn by the Princess Yun Chi. He shaved his promising beard and put whiting upon his cheeks, painted his eyebrows, and practiced a willowy walk. All in all, he made a fairish pretty maiden, and quite deceiving to the eye.

When the sun had snuggled down behind the mountains, Prince Ting Tsun walked in the palace gardens, taking those paths most favored by the princess. He fondled the delicate wistaria. He touched his face to the wide-expanded roses. Beneath the purple-flowered paulownia he paused in rapture. By look and action he was a maiden, taking her pleasure in the flowers.

Out of the calm evening air came a mighty and horrendous whistling roar. No need to tell the prince its cause. In his early days he had heard silly nurses attempt such a whistling, trying to frighten him into being "a good boy. If you don't,

By look and action he was a maiden.

the *loong* will get you." He had laughed at the
affronted nurses. But now . . . his face was
crinkled with grim lines, serious lines that spelled
determination. Not a trace of laughter there. The
whistling changed to a hissing. The air became
noxious with hot breath. Four tremendous padded
talons enfolded Prince Ting Tsun. A scream of
terror. A whanging of wings that lifted . . . Gone
. . . Vanished.

A scream of terror? No, that is not true. It was a
scream of mock terror. Can you think the prince

was frightened? Prince Ting Tsun? He screamed merely to make his deception doubly sure. The prince to casual gaze was a maiden, and maidens are supposed to scream when snapped up by a dragon. Small blame to them for that.

Up . . . Higher . . . Swifter . . . Up through the uncharted, the star-littered spaces swept Prince Ting Tsun, borne by the dragon. The wind shrieked past him. Higher, still higher. The little stars twinkled above. Higher . . . The little stars twinkled below. The air grew thin and cold. Prince Ting grew faint, for his breathing was of no consequence. There was no air to breathe. There was nothing but space and star dust.

The *loong*'s mouth went wide in a whinnying whistle. From close by came an answer. The prince opened his eyes. He saw a tapering streak of flame. On earth he would have named it "comet." But, stretching his eyes wider, he perceived that it was merely another dragon, its fiery breath trailing, far spread. Other *loongs* appeared; Ting Tsun imagined that he must be approaching their lair. He prayed that his arm might be strong.

With another scream the dragon folded his wings and dropped lightly upon a silvery plain. The journey was done—the moon underfoot.

The dragon King ruled in a subterranean

A whanging of wings that lifted. . . . Up . . .
Higher . . . Swifter.

palace. The entrance was merely a shining smooth hole, but the interior was luxury itself, with brocaded tapestries and jade floorings and translucent moonstone ceilings. In the throne room knelt Ting Tsun before the King—for he still played the part of a maiden. He knelt as if seeking mercy.

"Her beauty is not what I expected," growled the King. "Take her away. Perhaps another day she will seem fairer. Let her food be sesame and coriander seeds. Ugh. What a clumsy walk."

Prince Ting Tsun sat on a couch, turning in his mind a plan by which to vanquish his captors. The stillness was dissolved by a music of moving silks. A smiling damsel bowed before His Highness.

"Oh, I am glad to see that you do not weep like the others. Are you a princess from the earth or from *chin hsing?*" (Venus)

"From the earth," replied Ting Tsun, but he forgot to gentle his voice. The Moon Maiden shrank back.

"You are *not* a princess," she accused.

"No, I am not a princess. These garments are a deceit. I *was* Prince Ting Tsun, when upon the earth. Now I am Chang Pan—your slave."

The Moon Maiden was quickly reassured, and entered into talk with Ting Tsun, or humble Chang Pan, as he then called himself. She told the prince that she had lived with her parents on the far side of the moon—until the dragons came. Now she had no parents. And when the feast season of Brightest Light arrived, the dragon King (Chao Ya, his name) would make her his bride. She knew the number of dragons—twenty-eight, one for each night in the month, and there was never more than one home at a given time. They could be slain only with the dragon King's sword—a weapon that could slay the King himself. But—and the hopes of Prince Ting fell as she spoke—the King always kept the sword fastened at his waist. Yes, the *loong* King sometimes slept, but never more than once a day, and never for more than a few minutes. When? Just as the moon went down.

So Ting Tsun in his spotless maiden garb came upon the King asleep, and snatching up the Monarch's sword, awoke him and slew him. The blade had not yet done its sweep when it cleft the skull of a dragon who should have been guarding his King from harm.

The prince rejoiced at his success, howbeit rather modestly. His task had but started. There was many a chance for disaster. Death might lurk in a faltering blow, a lagging step, a momentary closing of the eyes.

By day the prince slept. By night he kept his post at the palace entrance. As each *loong* came crawling into his lair, Prince Ting Tsun reached its heart with the dragon King's sword. One thrust for each *loong*. One thrust each night, until a month had passed. In such manner His Valiant Highness destroyed the whole vile brood. His plans had carried through to triumph. Now he was free to return home and claim for his own the Princess Yun Chi. And a happy day it would be. He was happy now . . . oh, extremely happy. . . . Why shouldn't he be happy? the prince argued stoutly with himself. Yet his argument was not convincing. He would be compelled to leave the Moon Maiden. So his reasoning was hollow. He was not happy. He was sorrowful. He had grown fond of the Other World Princess.

But he must return to his own country. King Chan Ko had promised his daughter to whosoever should slay the dragon. In taking up battle, Prince Ting had given agreement to the terms. He was betrothed to the Princess Yun Chi.

The Moon Maiden was asleep when Prince Ting went to say good-bye. He would not wake her. He would go at once—after a last sad look. The sleeping princess stirred in her sleep, and murmured. For another instant the royal youth paused. He heard his name murmured. He heard more— enough to amaze him, to weaken his will almost to the changing point. A moment more of listening, and Prince Ting Tsun must inevitably have remained upon the moon. But he would hear no more. He rushed from the palace, ashamed of his weakness, yet thrilled with pride.

The moon hung low above the eastern ocean when Ting Tsun made his fearsome leap. He descended in the cushioning waters, and so took no hurt. Fortune was with him in that leap. A vessel, manned by venturesome explorers, chanced upon him. Otherwise, the spot where he fell must have been his grave, for ships are years apart in that faraway region. The sailors drew him aboard their junk and treated him with every respect. It was quite clear in their minds that he must be a god—certainly, he could be nothing less than a great magician.

When the ship touched at Ma Kao, Prince Ting Tsun was the first to step ashore. He found the city celebrating, burning much colored paper to the ruler of Married Happiness, feasting and making music. Accosting a stranger, he asked the cause of such jubilation, explaining that he had only that moment arrived from a far country.

The stranger answered: "We celebrate a marriage, Your Grace; Prince Yen has taken the fairest bride in all the world. From what country do you come?"

"Whom did Prince Yen marry?" asked Ting Tsun.

"Why, the Princess Yun Chi, of course. What country did you say?"

"Indeed?" exclaimed the prince. "And I came from the moon." Leaving the fellow with eyes popped and mouth agape, he hastened on. He was compelled to hasten. His feet would keep step with his tumultuous heart. So the Princess Yun Chi was married. King Chan Ko had broken his word. Far better if Prince Ting had remained upon the moon. Upon the moon was one who . . .

Pausing only for momentary snatches of sleep, Prince Ting journeyed the straightest road to Kwen Lun Mountain. On this mountain lived, and lives, the friendly mother demon, Si Wang, a magician of great power. To her, Prince Ting gave his necessary oath, and in exchange received his desire—wings feathered from the pinions of a phoenix.

The way is long. The way is steep. But hearts must be served. With wings unfaltering, Prince Ting Tsun cleaves the sky. Between the earth and the lighted moon his shadow may be seen— nearing the silvered plain, and the palace, and the princess . . . Prince Ting Tsun returning to his Maiden of the Moon.

Ah Tcha the Sleeper

Years ago, in southern China, lived a boy, Ah Tcha by name. Ah Tcha was an orphan, but not according to rule. A most peculiar orphan was he. It is usual for orphans to be very, very poor. That is the world-wide custom. Ah Tcha, on the contrary, was quite wealthy. He owned seven farms, with seven times seven horses to draw the plow. He owned seven mills, with plenty of breezes to spin them. Furthermore, he owned seven thousand pieces of gold, and a fine white cat.

The farms of Ah Tcha were fertile, were wide. His horses were brisk in the furrow. His mills never lacked for grain, nor wanted for wind. And his gold was good sharp gold, with not so much as a trace of copper. Surely, few orphans have been better provided for than the youth named Ah Tcha. And what a busy person was this Ah Tcha! His bed was always cold when the sun arose. Early in the morning he went from field to field, from mill to mill, urging on the people who worked for him. The setting sun always found him on his feet, hastening from here to there, persuading his laborers to more gainful efforts. And the moon of midnight often discovered him pushing up and down the little teakwood balls of a counting board, or else threading cash, placing coins upon a string. Eight farms, nine farms, he owned, and more stout horses. Ten mills, eleven, another white cat. It was Ah Tcha's ambition to become the richest person in the world.

They who worked for the wealthy orphan were inclined now and then to grumble. Their pay was not beggarly, but how they did toil to earn that pay which was not beggarly! It was go, and go, and go. Said the ancient woman Nu Wu, who worked with a rake in the field: "Our master drives us as if he were a fox and we were hares in the open. Round the field and round and round, hurry, always hurry." Said Hu Shu, her husband, who bound the grain into sheaves: "Not hares, but horses. We are driven like the horses of Lung Kuan, who . . ." It's a long story.

But Ah Tcha, approaching the murmurers, said, "Pray be so good as to hurry, most excellent Nu Wu, for the clouds gather blackly, with thunder." And to the scowling husband he said, "Speed your work, I beg you, Honorable Hu Shu, for the grain must be under shelter before the smoke of Evening Rice ascends."

When Ah Tcha had eaten his Evening Rice, he took a lantern and entered the largest of his mills. A scampering rat drew his attention to the floor. There he beheld no less than a score of rats, some gazing at him as if undecided whether to flee or continue the feast, others gnawing—and who are you, nibbling and caring not? And only a few short whisker lengths away sat an enormous cat, sleeping the sleep of a mossy stone. The cat was black in color, black as a crow's wing dipped in pitch, upon a night of inky darkness. That describes her coat. Her face was somewhat more black. Ah Tcha had never before seen her. She was not his cat. But his or not, he thought it a trifle unreasonable of her to sleep while the rats held high carnival. The rats romped between her paws. Still she slept. It angered Ah Tcha. The lantern rays fell on her eyes. Still she slept. Ah Tcha grew more and more provoked. He decided then and there to teach the cat that his mill was no place for sleepyheads.

*When Ah Tcha had eaten his Evening Rice, he took
a lantern and entered the largest of his mills.*

Accordingly, he seized an empty grain sack and hurled it with such exact aim that the cat was sent heels over head. "There, old Crouch-by-the-Hole," said Ah Tcha in a tone of wrath. "Remember your paining ear, and be more vigilant." But the cat had no sooner regained her feet than she changed into . . . Nu Wu . . . changed into Nu Wu, the old woman who worked in the fields . . . a witch. What business she had in the mill is a puzzle. However, it is undoubtedly true that mills hold grain, and grain is worth money. And that may be an explanation. Her sleepiness is no puzzle at all. No wonder she was sleepy, after working so hard in the field, the day's length through.

The anger of Nu Wu was fierce and instant. She wagged a crooked finger at Ah Tcha, screeching: "Oh, you cruel moneygrubber. Because you fear the rats will eat a pennyworth of grain, you must beat me with bludgeons. You make me work like a slave all day—and wish me to work all night. You beat me and disturb my slumber. Very well, since you will not let me sleep, I shall cause you to slumber eleven hours out of every dozen. . . . Close your eyes." She swept her wrinkled hand across Ah Tcha's face. Again taking the form of a cat, she bounded downstairs.

She had scarce reached the third step descending

when Ah Tcha felt a compelling desire for sleep. It was as if he had taken gum of the white poppy flower, as if he had tasted honey of the gray moon blossom. Eyes half closed, he stumbled into a grain bin. His knees doubled beneath him. Down he went, curled like a dormouse. Like a dormouse he slumbered.

From that hour began a change in Ah Tcha's fortune. The spell gripped him fast. Nine-tenths of his time was spent in sleep. Unable to watch over his laborers, they worked when they pleased, which was seldom. They idled when so inclined— and that was often, and long. Furthermore, they stole in a manner most shameful. Ah Tcha's mills became empty of grain. His fields lost their fertility. His horses disappeared—strayed, so it was said. Worse yet, the unfortunate fellow was summoned to a magistrate's *yamen,* there to defend himself in a lawsuit. A neighbor declared that Ah Tcha's huge black cat had devoured many chickens. There were witnesses who swore to the deed. They were sure, one and all, that Ah Tcha's black cat was the cat at fault. Ah Tcha was sleeping too soundly to deny that the cat was his. . . . So the magistrate could do nothing less than make the cat's owner pay damages, with all costs of the lawsuit.

Thereafter, trials at court were a daily occurrence. A second neighbor said that Ah Tcha's black cat had stolen a flock of sheep. Another complained that the cat had thieved from him a herd of fattened bullocks. Worse and worse grew the charges. And no matter how absurd, Ah Tcha, sleeping in the prisoner's cage, always lost and had to pay damages. His money soon passed into other hands. His mills were taken from him. His farms went to pay for the lawsuits. Of all his wide lands, there remained only one little acre—and it was grown up in worthless bushes. Of all his goodly buildings, there was left one little hut, where the boy spent most of his time, in witch-imposed slumber.

Now, near by in the mountain of Huge Rocks Piled, lived a greatly ferocious *loong,* or, as foreigners would say, a dragon. This immense beast, from tip of forked tongue to the end of his shadow, was far longer than a barn. With the exception of length, he was much the same as any other *loong.* His head was shaped like that of a camel. His horns were deer horns. He had bulging rabbit eyes, a snake neck. Upon his many ponderous feet were tiger claws, and the feet were shaped very like sofa cushions. He had walrus whiskers, and a breath of red-and-blue flame. His voice was like the sound of a hundred brass kettles pounded. Black fish scales covered his body; black feathers grew upon his limbs. Because of his color he was sometimes called *Oo Loong*. From that it would seem that *Oo* means neither white nor pink.

The black *loong* was not regarded with any great esteem. His habit of eating a man—two men if they were little—every day made him rather unpopular. Fortunately, he prowled only at night. Those folk who went to bed decently at nine o'clock had nothing to fear. Those who rambled well along toward midnight often disappeared with a sudden and complete thoroughness.

As everyone knows, cats are much given to night skulking. The witch-cat Nu Wu was no exception. Midnight often found her miles afield. On such a midnight, when she was roving in the form of a hag, what should approach but the black dragon. Instantly the *loong* scented prey, and instantly he made for the old witch.

There followed such a chase as never was before on land or sea. Up hill and down dale, by stream and wood and fallow, the cat woman flew and the dragon coursed after. The witch soon failed of breath. She panted. She wheezed. She stumbled on a bramble, and a claw slashed through her garments. Too close for comfort. The harried witch

changed shape to a cat, and bounded off afresh,
half a li at every leap. The *loong* increased his pace,
and soon was close behind, gaining. For a most
peculiar fact about the *loong* is that the more he
runs, the easier his breath comes and the swifter
grows his speed. Hence, it is not surprising that
his fiery breath was presently singeing the witch-
cat's back.

In a twinkling the cat altered form once more,
and as an old hag scuttled across a turnip field.
She was merely an ordinarily powerful witch. She
possessed only the two forms—cat and hag. Nor
did she have a gift of magic to baffle or cripple the
hungry black *loong*. Nevertheless, the witch was
not despairing. At the edge of the turnip field lay
Ah Tcha's miserable patch of thick bushes. So
thick were the bushes as to be almost a wall against
the hag's passage. As a hag, she could have no hope
of entering such a thicket. But as a cat, she could
race through without hindrance. And the dragon
would be sadly bothered in following. Scheming
thus, the witch dashed under the bushes—a cat
once more.

Ah Tcha was roused from slumber by the most
outrageous noise that had ever assailed his ears.
There was such a snapping of bushes, such an
awful bellowed screeching that even the dead of a
century must have heard. The usually sound-sleep-

ing Ah Tcha was awakened at the outset. He soon realized how matters stood—or ran. Luckily, he had learned of the only reliable method for frightening off the dragon. He opened his door and hurled a red, a green, and a yellow firecracker in the monster's path.

In through his barely opened door the witch-cat dragged her exhausted self. "I don't see why you couldn't open the door sooner," she scolded, changing into a hag. "I circled the hut three times before you had the gumption to let me in."

"I am very sorry, good Mother. I was asleep." From Ah Tcha.

"Well, don't be so sleepy again," scowled the witch, "or I'll make you suffer. Get me food and drink."

"Again, Honored Lady, I am sorry. So poor am I that I have only water for drink. My food is the leaves and roots of bushes."

"No matter. Get what you have and quickly."

Ah Tcha reached outside the door and stripped a handful of leaves from a bush. He plunged the leaves into a kettle of hot water, and signified that the meal was prepared. Then he lay down to doze, for he had been awake fully half a dozen minutes, and the desire to sleep was returning stronger every moment.

The witch soon supped and departed, without

leaving so much as half a "Thank you." When Ah Tcha awoke again, his visitor was gone. The poor boy flung another handful of leaves into his kettle, and drank quickly. He had good reason for haste. Several times he had fallen asleep with the cup at his lips—a most unpleasant situation, and scalding. Having taken several sips, Ah Tcha stretched him out for a resumption of his slumber. Five minutes passed . . . ten minutes . . . fifteen. . . . Still his eyes failed to close. He took a few more sips from the cup, and felt more awake than ever.

"I do believe," said Ah Tcha, "that she has thanked me by bewitching my bushes. She has charmed the leaves to drive away my sleepiness."

And so she had. Whenever Ah Tcha felt tired and sleepy—and at first that was often—he had only to drink of the bewitched leaves. At once his drowsiness departed. His neighbors soon learned of the bushes that banished sleep. They came to drink of the magic brew. There grew such a demand that Ah Tcha decided to set a price on the leaves. Still the demand continued. More bushes were planted. Money came.

Throughout the province people called for "the drink of Ah Tcha." In time they shortened it by asking for "Ah Tcha's drink," then for "Tcha's drink," and finally for "Tcha."

And that is its name at present, "Tcha," or "Tay," or "Tea," as some call it. And one kind of Tea is still called "Oo Loong"—"Black Dragon."

I Wish It Would Rain

It rains and rains in Kiang Sing. And then it rains some more. No sooner is one cloud past than another comes treading on its heels. By day and by night the raindrops patter, and *ko tzu* from his lily pad croaks "More rain. More rain." Old men going to bed wear their *wei li* (rain hats), instead of tasseled nightcaps. Many young people have only a hazy idea as to what the word "sun" means. Pour and beat and drizzle, drizzle and drive with the gale. And that is Kiang Sing.

Three reasons are given by the people of Kiang Sing for their extremely weepy climate. Some say that the Shen Yu Shih, who lords it over the clouds, lives near by on the Daylight Mountain. Others are firm in their declaration that Moo Yee, the mighty archer, and a naughty fellow withal, shot the sky above Kiang Sing full of arrow holes. Naturally, a sky full of arrow holes is bound to leak. There are still others, and very learned folk among them, who declare that Mei Li, weeping for her lost hero, Wei Sheng, is responsible for the torrents. Dear only knows which is the correct theory. It may be that all three are to blame. The only certainty is that Kiang Sing has a very heavy rainfall and that Tiao Fu lived there and learned to love wet weather. . . . *To love it?* She hated it.

Tiao Fu was a very pretty maiden—no gainsaying that. She had the most wonderful black long hair in all Kiang Sing. But beauty was her one and only possession. She had no skill with the needle, whether to sew or embroider. Her cooking was more than a disgrace. When her fingers touched the *pi pa,* that usually sweet-toned instrument gave out a demon's wail. She could not even smooth a quilt on the *kang.* The beds were all hills and hollows. How could she make beds when her hair needed burnishing? She scarce knew which end of a broom was meant for the floor. How could she sweep when her hair required glossing? New matting would cover the floor's disarray. Tiao Fu smoothed her hair, and dreamed of the time when she would marry a rich mandarin and be carried in glory away from Kiang Sing and its terrible rains. The hateful rains of Kiang Sing.

No wonder her father, Ching Chi, became so poverty-stricken. Gradually his fortune slipped away until his only property was the large and

How could she make beds when her hair needed burnishing?

poorly furnished, extremely ill-kept house in which he lived. Even so, this house when viewed from the street appeared superior to its fellows. It was the handsomest and most considerable *yamen* in Pin Jen Village.

The size and appearance of the *yamen* accounts for what happened. One fiendish night, in a mighty drumming of rain, there came a more noisy drumming of maces upon Ching Chi's door. "Open, in the King's name!" commanded voices outside. Forthwith Ching Chi flung open the door. He beheld runners dressed in the royal livery, and in their hands the gold-banded staves of their authority. "Prepare to receive and entertain the illustrious person of Ho Chu the King. His Most Gracious Majesty will arrive *sha shih chien* [within a slight shower's time]. Therefore prepare. It is a command."

Far from entertaining royalty, old Ching Chi had never so much as glimpsed a King. Heart and knees failed him utterly. He could only grovel upon the floor and mutter weakly of his unworthiness. Tiao Fu, however, was not so deeply affected. A King? Let him enter. Say what you please, kings are mortal men. No food in the house? *Ya ya pei* (pish, pooh). And the tradesmen refused all credit? What of it? No tradesman in his senses would refuse a bargain. And what would the bargain be?

Tiao Fu snatched up her little-used embroidery scissors. Snip. Snip. Snip. Down fell a cataract of her long black hair. Snip. Snip. Again and again. The hair that was her vanity lay upon the floor. Her lustrous hair—sacrified—to make a feast for the King. Hastily donning her father's *wei li,* she dashed from the house. There was no trouble in making a bargain. The tradesman's first offer was almost within reason, and Tiao Fu had no time to wrangle. She bartered her hair for cooked fowls and rice and all that goes to make a dinner.

*Tiao Fu snatched up her little-used embroidery scis-
sors. Snip. Snip. Snip.*

I Wish It Would Rain

King Ho Chu arrived betimes. The weather despite, he was in good spirit. He was such a considerate and jolly Monarch that he soon had old Ching Chi at perfect ease. The dinner was a delight to eye and tongue. It was the best meal that had been served in Ching Chi's home for many a moon. And Tiao Fu's hair had bought it.

After the cups were turned down, King Ho Chu inquired about his horse. To reiterate, he was a most considerate sovereign. He wished to feel sure that his steed was housed from the rain, and shoulder deep in a well-filled manger. Ching Chi beamingly affirmed that the horse had been provided for, lavishly. What else *could* he say? However, he would make sure, doubly sure, by going to the stable again.

Of course, the poor horse had not a mouthful. There was not so much as a wisp of hay in the stable, not so much as a bean or a stalk. Ching Chi was sunk in weepy despair when the girl Taio Fu appeared with a matting from her bedroom floor. It was a newly made matting, of bright clean straw. Tiao Fu tore it into shreds and filled the manger heaping. Thus was the King's horse supplied with food—food none too nourishing, but food nevertheless.

There are many channels through which kings

may receive news and rumors and tittle-tattle.
What with the secret police and the mandarins
who wish to gain favor, and the—the sparrows—
the royal palace keeps well informed. (Besides,
one historian takes several pages to prove that
Tiao Fu possessed a tongue and could use it to her
advantage.) However that may be, the news
spread. Within a day King Ho Chu learned how
the maid Tiao Fu had provided a feast at the
expense of her hair. He learned all about the
shredded matting, and his laughter shook the
throne. He bestowed more than a passing thought
upon Tiao Fu of the quaintly bobbed locks—the
maiden a thousand years ahead of her time. And
having thought—he acted. He said to the Minister
of Domestic Affairs, "Prepare a room with hang-
ings of orange-colored silk." To the Minister of
the Treasury he said, "Bestow a dozen or so bars
of gold upon the mandarin Ching Chi." The Minister of Matrimony received his command,
"Arrange me a wedding with the maid Tiao Fu, of
Kiang Sing." So all things were arranged and
came to pass.

King Ho Chu was well pleased. Old Ching Chi
was the happiest man living. The maid Tiao Fu
was quite content—for a space. She had gowns of
gorgeousness undreamed. She had slaves to kneel

and knock their heads whenever she beckoned. She had priceless jewels and food of the rarest. Incidentally, she had in the King a doting husband. She had everything—everything—except rain. . . .

Is it not hard to believe that Tiao Fu grew homesick for the rains of Kiang Sing? It is a strain upon belief, yet it is true, indubitably. Tiao Fu longed for the rains of her drenched and soggy much be-drizzled Kiang Sing. Did the King present her with a new necklace—she threw it petulantly away, exclaiming that she wanted rain— "Oh, I wish it would rain," said Tiao Fu. "Why don't you make it rain?" "Then I will," said the King. He installed a myriad of high-spouting fountains, at no slight drain to the treasury. "Are you pleased, my beauteous Tiao Fu?" "No," fretfully. "It is not like the rains of Kiang Sing. Why are the trees not green? The trees are bare and brown. Oh, I wish it would rain—a green-bringing rain."

The trees might very well be bare and brown. Winter's greedy fingers had stripped them thoroughly. King Ho Chu gazed at the barren limbs for a lengthy period before his mind hit upon a scheme for bringing back the green. At length he summoned the royal tailor and to him said: "Take many bales of green-colored silk and cut leaf-shaped pieces. Dip the pieces in wax; then sew

". . . and cut leaf-shaped pieces."

them upon those bare branches. And use such artistry that no eye can discover they are not true leaves. *Tsu po"* (Be quick). The *cheng i* (make clothes) hastily employed all the city's master workmen, some cutting and many sewing. Overnight the trees took on a color. Indeed, the tailor went beyond his orders, for on the peach trees he sewed lovely pink blossoms. And some blossoms he tacked to the ground—as if in their ripeness they had fallen.

For a few days Tiao Fu was in somewhat better humor. Once, she actually smiled. But all too soon those few days were over, and her crossness returned. "What now, my pearl of southern seas?" said the King. "Have the leaves lost their freshness? Do they no longer please?" "Oh [pout], it isn't the leaves. They are quite homelike. It's the wind that I miss. I long to hear the shrieking wind of Kiang Sing, hurling its rain against my lattice. Oh, I wish it would rain.''

Poor King Ho Chu was hard put. Wind? Wind? . . . By the uprooted pine tree of Mount Tai, how was he to produce the wind. A good half hour— sixty minutes in that land—passed before he had an inspiration. Again he called for the royal tailor. ''Procure,'' he told the tailor, ''many bales of the stoutest silk. Then place some of your brawniest men outside yonder lattice, and have them rip the silk, tear it into strips—with all the noise possible.'' With which, King Ho Chu entered the treasury to see how his gold was dwindling.

Huge-armed stalwarts stood outside Tiao Fu's window. Their hands clutched the woven silk. A pull. ''Sh-r-r-r-r-iek. Pull. Sh-r-r-r-r-iek.'' For two days the brow of Tiao Fu was smooth and untroubled. She actually spoke kindly to the King. He, poor soul, didn't hear it. He was too busy wondering what the next task would be, and how expensive.

Scarcely a hundred bales of silk had been torn when Tiao Fu hurled her crown across the room and began to weep. ''My dear, what's the trouble? What *is* the trouble?'' questioned Ho Chu. ''Is the wind too violent?'' ''Oh, no. The wind is natural enough, and it pleases me. I miss—oh, how I *do* miss the rumbling thunder of Kiang Sing, and the fall of lightning-shattered trees. I miss them and, oh, I wish it would rain—real rain." The tears fell faster with each word.

Now King Ho Chu had a tremendous army encamped on the palace grounds. He summoned General Chang and explained matters—with an order. No sooner ordered than accomplished. The soldiers in their heaviest shoes marched ponderously beneath the latticed window. "Boom. Boom. Bru-u-u-um. Bru-u-u-um. Bru-u-u-u-ump." And how do you like our thunder? Little drums and great, they rattled and roared. "Rap-p-p. Boom. Boom. . . ." In endless line the soldiers marched. One day. Two days. Three days. Four. Some of them slept while the others marched. Boom. Boom. Boom. The sun on their spears blazed and flickered —the lightning. By night there were flashing fires.

It is gratifying to relate that Tiao Fu was moderately pleased. Her appetite returned and the tears were withheld. She spoke to the King with kindness—several times. All might have gone well had not some malcontents down Kan Su way started a rebellion. Off went the army—General Chang waving his sword, and the smallest drummer boy thumping with glee. That was at midnight.

The dawn was at its breaking when beacons along the line of march flared up. "Halt" was the signal. The army halted. Again the beacons flared. They spelled the word "Return."

Tiao Fu was not so well. She longed for the roll of the drums to remind her of Kiang Sing's thunder. What could the poor King do but recall his army? The rebellion in Kan Su continued merrily. And General Chang, who was an old-time soldier, expressed his opinion—rather explosively—to a sympathetic staff officer. But never mind that. Let the drums sound.

When the rebellion spread to Kan Si, the King felt that things had gone quite far enough. It was time to teach those rebels a lesson. Away went the army again.

A whole day passed, and no return order was signaled. Night came, and the army tramped onward. . . . A pillar of flame shot up from a hilltop. It was a beacon. "Return," said the beacon. "Not I," said General Chang; "I've had enough of the Queen's whims. Besides, it's raining right now. Forward, march."

The army entered Kan Su and there encountered the rebels. It is better that the fight go undescribed. Here suffice it to say that if so much as one rebel escaped, he took pains to keep the fact

169

secret. There is no mention of him in the books.

General Chang was jubilant. Surely the King would be highly pleased. The King—good gracious—King Ho Chu himself, on a breathless steed, stumbled across the battlefield. "Why didn't you return?" panted the King. "I—I—I—" stammered General Chang. But the King said more. "The Tartars swooped down just a few hours ago, carrying off my Queen, raiding my treasury (though it was empty), and forcing me to flee for my life. They carried off the Queen."

"How terrible!" exclaimed General Chang, looking into his sleeve. "And my army is so tired that it can't march a step—besides, the roads will soon be *pu neng chu* [can't go] with the rain."

High as Han Hsin

Han Hsin was not at all high as to stature. He was short, short as a day in the Month of Long Nights. But as a leader of bow-drawing men, his place is high. As inventor of the world's first kite, he rose very high indeed, and that accounts for the saying "High as Han Hsin."

The night that saw Han Hsin's birth was no ordinary night. It was a night of fear and grandeur. The Shen who places the stars in the sky had a shaking hand that eve. His fingers were palsied and could not hold. Star after star dropped down toward earth, and the people prayed and wept, the while they exploded firecrackers. It's a sinister sign when the stars tumble out of the sky. This the people knew. Therefore, they trembled.

But amid the falling stars was one that rose, as

if the Shen had tossed it, as if the Shen had thrown it high. One large star mounted higher and higher the while its companions fell. Wise men, astrologers, they who scan the heavens, said: "The stars that fall are mighty men who die. The star that rises—that is the star of a future great man—born this night."

The wise men of the village kept careful watch over Han Hsin. He had been born on the night of the Rising Star. They thought perhaps he might be the ward of the Star. They watched closely for signs to strengthen their belief. But for some years Han Hsin disappointed them. He rattled his calabash in an extremely ordinary manner. There was no hint of greatness in the way he bounced a ball. Yet the astrologers held to their faith, and watched—and finally were rewarded.

There came a rain, not a hard rain, nevertheless a wetting rain, sufficient to drive the villagers under shelter. But Han Hsin remained in the open where quick drops pelted. A foolish villager noticed him and said, laughing: "Look you at our future great man. He knows not enough to seek cover from the storm. Ho. Ho. Ho. How wise."

An old astrologer said: "Hush, *Chieh Kuo* [Dunce]; do you not see that the youth makes a bridge? Come with me." They went closer to have a more complete view. The flowing water had formed a little island in the street. Upon the island were many ants. As the water rose, the island grew smaller—and the number of ants grew smaller, many being swept away to their death. Han Hsin raised a bridge from island to mainland. The ants quickly discovered his bridge and crossed to safety. "It is a sign," said the old astrologer, "*Chi li* [a good omen]. He has befriended the ants. The ants will remember. Someday they will do him an equal service—helping him to become great."

Han Hsin raised a bridge from island to mainland.

Han Hsin discovered in the King's paved road a hatchet of better than fair metal. None of the villagers could prove ownership. Little Han was permitted to keep his treasure. Quite soon a spirited chopping was heard—steel ringing upon stone. A foolish villager said: "Look. Han Hsin uses his fine hatchet to chop the old millstone—thus demonstrating his great genius. Ho. Ho. Ho. He uses valuable edged steel to chip stone."

The old astrologer said, "Hush, *Sha Tzu* [Imbecile]; come with me, and behold." A worn-out millstone lay at the edge of the road. Through the hole in its center grew a bamboo tree. The hole was small. Already it hindered the tree's growth. Retarded as it was, the bamboo could never reach a full growth. Han Hsin belabored the stone till it split in two pieces. Then there was plenty of room for the tree. There was nothing to "pull its elbow."

"That is good," asserted the astrologer. "He saves the bamboo from death. Someday the bamboo will reward him—help him to become great."

Shortly afterward, the astrologer gave Han Hsin a note of recommendation to the King. Han went to the King, seeking employ. He wished a command in the army. But His Majesty was in a sulky mood and would not see the boy. Therefore, Han continued his journey into Chin Chou, a neighboring country. He went to the ruler, Prince Chin, and exhibited his note. The prince read—and laughed. "You are too small to serve in my army. My soldiers are giants, all—very strong. You—are *Ko Tsao* [Little hopping insect]. No." Han solemnly declared that his strength was that of a river in flood, and begged for a trial. "Well, if you are determined," said the prince, "take my spear and raise it above your head." The prince's spear was solid iron from point to heel, and longer than the mast of a sea-venturing junk. Furthermore, it had been greased with tiger fat to prevent rust. Han grasped the spear to raise it. His fingers slipped. Down crashed the heavy weapon. "Take whips and lash him out of the city—clumsy knave that he is!" Prince Chin roared in a great voice—angrily. The spear had missed His Royal Person by the merest mite.

An old councilor spoke: "Your Highness, surely it cannot be that you intend to let the rogue live? He will someday return with an army to take revenge." "Nonsense," said the prince. "He is no more than an ant—and idiotic besides. How could such a fellow secure an army?" "Nevertheless, I fear the ant will work your downfall. He must be killed." The councilor insisted. He argued so strongly for Han's death that, rather than hear more, the prince consented. "It is useless. But do as you wish. Send a squad of horse to overtake him and fetch back his head."

When Han Hsin beheld the soldiers approaching at top speed, there was no doubt in his mind as to what harsh errand brought them. He knew they intended to have his head. But Han, having lived so long with his head, had become fond of it, and preferred to keep it on his shoulders. But how? How could it be saved? There was no escape by running. There was no place to hide. The boy must use his wits.

Hastily tying a cord to his bamboo staff, he threw the staff into a tiny shallow puddle of water that lay beside the road. The soldiers galloped up to find him seated on the bank—fishing—and weeping. "And what ails you, simpleton?" a soldier asked. "Have you lost your nurse?" Between sobs Han answered, "I am hungry and I can't catch any fish." "What a booby!" said another soldier. "He fishes in a puddle no larger than a copper cash." "Look," said yet another, "he throws in the pole, and holds the hook in his hand. What a *chieh kuo;* as foolish as Nu Wa, who melted stones to mend a hole in the sky. Do you suppose this is the creature we were told to kill?" He was answered: "Nonsense. Prince Chin doesn't send his cavalry to kill an ant. Spur your horses."

When the troops returned and reported their lack of success, there was much talk. The councilor raged, offering to resign. He was positive that so long as Han Hsin lived, the government would be in danger. He was bitter because the troops had mistaken Han's cunning for imbecility. Merely to humor the councilor, Prince Chin mounted a horse and galloped away with his troops.

Han Hsin put his best foot foremost, hurrying toward the border. He longed to trudge the turf of his own country once more. It was not that homesickness urged his steps. Han felt reasonably sure that his friends, the soldiers, would shortly take the road again. The next time they might not be so easily deluded. Therefore, he hastened. But it was useless. His own country was still miles distant when he beheld the dust of men who whipped their horses.

It is not pleasant to have one's head lopped off. At times it is almost annoying. Han thought quickly. Near by was a melon patch. The melons were large in their ripeness. Upon a huge striped *hsi kua* the boy sat him down and wept. The tears coursed down his cheeks, and his body shook with sobbing. Undoubtedly, his sorrow was great.

Prince Chin stopped his steed with a jerk. *"Ai chi*—such grief. Are you trying to drown yourself with tears?" "I—I—I am hungry," stammered

"I—I—I—am hungry," stammered Han Hsin.

Han Hsin. "Hungry? Then why don't you eat a melon?" "I would, sire, but I've lost my knife. So I must s-s-starve." The prince was well assured that he had met with the most foolish person in the world. "What? Starve because you have no knife? . . . Strike the melon with a stone. . . . Such a dunce. It would never do for me to behead this fellow. The Shen who watches over imbeciles would be made angry." A trooper slashed a dozen melons with his sword. Surely a dozen would save the idiot from starvation. Oh, what an idiot!

Han Hsin sat on the ground, obscuring his features in the red heart of a melon as the prince and his men departed. His lips moved—but not in eating. His lips moved in silent laughter.

Han Hsin bothered no more Kings with notes setting forth the argument that he had been born under a lucky star, and so deserved well. Quite casually, he fell in with King Kao Lin's army. He received no pay. His name was not on the muster. He hobnobbed with all the soldiers and soon became a favorite. The boy had a remarkable memory. He learned the name of every soldier in the army. Further, he learned the good and bad traits of each soldier, knew who could be depended upon and who was unreliable. He knew from what village each man came, and he could describe the village with exactness. All from hearing the soldiers talk.

A fire destroyed the army muster roll. Han Hsin quickly wrote a new list, giving the name of each man, his age, his qualities, his parents, and his village. King Kao Lin marveled. Shortly afterward, he added Han's name to the list—a general.

Prince Chin made war upon King Kao Lin. He marched three armies through the kingdom, and where the armies had passed there was desolation, and no two stalks of grain remained in any field. Han Hsin moved against the smallest of the three armies. The enemy waited, well hidden above a mountain pass through which Han must march. It was an excellent ambush—there was no other passage. The mountain was so steep no man could climb it.

Han caused his soldiers to remove their jackets and fill them with sand, afterward tying bottom and top securely. The sandbags were placed against a cliff, to form a stairway. Up went Han and his men, to come upon the enemy from behind and capture the whole army—cook and general.

The second hostile army retreated to the river Lan Shui. It crossed the river, then burned all boats and bridges. So safe from pursuit felt the hostile general, he neglected to post sentries. Instead, he ordered all the men to feast and make pleasure. Han Hsin ordered his men to remove the iron points from their spears. The hollow bamboo shafts of the spears were lashed together, forming rafts. Armed only with light bows, the men quickly crossed Lan Shui River and pounced upon their unready enemy. The feast was eaten by soldiers other than those for whom it had been intended.

Prince Chin led the third and largest army. He had far more braves than Han commanded. There could be no whipping him in open battle. In strategy lay the only hope. Han Hsin clothed many thousand scarecrows and placed them in the battle line—a scarecrow, a soldier—another scarecrow, another soldier. In that manner, to all appearance, he doubled his army. Forthwith, he wrote a letter demanding surrender—pointing out that since his army was so much larger than Chin Pa's, to fight would be a useless sacrifice.

Prince Chin took long to decide upon his course. So long it took him that Han grew impatient and sat down to write again. While he wrote, a strong wind broke upon the camp. The papers on Han's table were lifted high in air. Higher and higher they swirled, higher than an eagle—for the Shen of Storms to read. Han's golden knife, resting on a paper, was lifted by the wind, transported far over the foeman's camp.

Immediately an idea seethed in the leader's mind. If a small piece of paper could carry a knife, might not a large piece carry the knife's owner? Especially when that owner happened to be not much more weighty than a three-day bean cake? It seemed reasonable. Again the little general took spears from his soldiers. The iron points were removed and the long bamboo shafts were bound together in a frame. Over the frame was fastened tough bamboo paper in many sheets. Away from prying enemy eyes, the queer contrivance was sent into the air. It proved skyworthy, lifting its maker to a fearsome height. Thus was the *feng cheng* invented. Thus was the kite, little brother of the airplane, invented by Han Hsin.

The night showed no moon. Not a star had been

lighted. The wind blew strong, with an eerie whistling. It was such a night as demons walk about their mischief, and honest men keep under their quilts. Out of the sky above the enemy camp came a great flapping sound. Could it be a dragon? All eyes peered upward through the darkness. . . . Two red eyes appeared. . . . Nothing more could be seen. . . . Only the two evil eyes. A voice came from the sky. "Return to your homes," boomed the voice. "The battle is lost. Return to your homes, ere they too are lost." The men of Chin shook with their fear. The Shen of the Sky had spoken. They had heard his voice. They had heard the flapping of his wings. They had seen his red and terrible eyes. How could the men of Chin know that the words they heard were uttered by Han Hsin? How could they know that the flapping was caused by a man-made thing, later to be named *"feng cheng"* (kite)? And how could they know that the eyes were mere bottles filled with insects called "Bright at night" (Fireflies)? The men of Chin could not know. They loosened the ropes of their tents—and the tents came down.

Prince Chin tried in vain to hold his followers. No longer followers were they. They were fugitives, fleeing to their homes. Only a few hundred remained true to their prince. Doubly armed with

Prince Chin tried in vain to hold his followers.

the weapons that had been thrown away, they ascended a steep and rocky hill, there to make their last great fight.

But Han Hsin had anticipated just such action, and had prepared for it. Unseen, he had slipped through the enemy lines and climbed the hill. With a brush dipped in honey he wrote words upon a stone. As he wrote, came hungry ants. The ants came—to aid—and to feast. Soon the stone was black with a crawling multitude.

Prince Chin scaled the hill to its summit. Ten thousand swords could not dislodge him from those rocks. He would make the enemy pay a red price for success. . . . His gaze fell upon the rock. . . . He saw a host of ants forming characters that read "THE BATTLE IS LOST." His men also beheld, and they said: "The ant is wisest of all animals. Let us crawl in the dust, for we are conquered."

So Han Hsin victored over the three hostile armies. His country was invaded no more. In time it became really his country, for he ruled it—as a King—ruled it well. But now his wise rule is forgotten. He is remembered as the man who first made kites.

Contrary Chueh Chun

The most contrary man that ever drew a full dozen breaths was Chueh Chun, living in Tien Ting Village, thirty minutes by donkey, by up-and-down very bad road, north of the Great Wall, the far-famed Chinese Wall.

Queer Chueh Chun had been named Ma Tzu by his honorable parents. He had been named Ma Tzu, which means Face Rather Ugly. He himself changed his name to Chueh Chun, which means Absolutely Beautiful.

The good people of Tien Ting Village lived tidily in made houses, aboveground. Chueh Chun lived in a cave, a deep and winding fox den, belowground. Such of the neighbors as were permitted by law to wear hats wore little round hats on their heads. Chueh Chun wore hats on his feet. Moreover, he wore straw hats in winter, fur in summer. On his head perched an ancient sandal. He pretended that the arrangement was excellent. The sandal shaded his eyes, yet permitted his head to remain cool.

The neighbors when going upon long journeys commonly rode their shaggy mountain ponies. Chueh Chun when setting forth on an arduous trip—say fifty miles—was most likely to walk. But to go from his fox-lair home to the nest of his speckled hen, he invariably rode a little donkey.

Yu Yuch Ying, aunt to Chueh Chun, willed her obstinate nephew thirty thousand cash, just when his purse was at its flattest. The neighbors gathered round Chueh Chun to congratulate and envy him. Said they: "What a fortunate person are you, dear Chueh Chun! The thirty thousand cash that your late lamented Aunt Yu Yuch Ying left will set you up in noble style. A most opportune windfall was that. Plenty of luck you have."

But Chueh Chun nodded his head. He always nodded his head to show that he differed. "Quite the contrary," said Chueh Chun, "I fear me, Honorable Neighbors, that my aunt's bequest is an ill thing altogether. It is luck the worst. Thirty thousand cash are so heavy that I shall be compelled to make at least two trips to fetch them. Besides, the beggars will be annoying me without letup from break of day till I break their heads.

And think of thieves. The money will bring me ill, I am sure." And Chueh Chun laughed heartily, for that was his way of expressing sorrow.

However, Chueh Chun's excellent wife knew how to manage him. She said: "Quite right. If I were you, I wouldn't dream of going for the fortune. And I wouldn't once think of riding the donkey, not once." And she spoke as if she meant her words.

Therefore—upon his donkey—the contrary husband started for Tsun Pu, where his beloved aunt had lived and left riches. Immediately outside Tien Ting Village the traveler was forced to cross a river. The current was swift, and it washed the hat-shoes from Chueh Chun's feet. Down the stream swirled the hats, with their owner in splashy pursuit. The neighbors, who had gathered to bid old Contrary a fine journey, were loud in lamentation over his loss. They exclaimed, beating their breasts: "Oh, Chueh Chun, we are so sorry that you have lost your hat-shoes, so utterly sorry. With our eyes we weep for you and cry 'alas.' What terrible luck. It is demon-sent luck in truth."

But Chueh Chun paused in his splashing, and answered them: "Why, no. I dare say it is not bad luck at all. Quite the opposite, my esteemed

Therefore—upon his donkey—the contrary husband started for Tsun Pu.

neighbors, it may be very fortunate indeed.'' He wept to show that he was well pleased.

Meanwhile, the onward swept hat-shoes disappeared from view. Chueh Chun raced along the bank, calling, and anxiously scanning the water for a trace of his lost property. The neighbors, too, hurried after, one leading the donkey. Rounding a willow-draped elbow of the river, Chueh Chun stumbled over a boat that had drifted ashore. He fell headlong and heavily, his chin plowing a prodigious furrow in the sand. Up panted the neighbors, shouting: "Alas, likewise alack. What woe! Such woe. Poor Chueh Chun, how we ache for you. Our own bones pain out of sympathy. What a horrible calamity!"

Chueh Chun stretched out a hand to pick up his two hat-shoes, drifted against a willow bough. Said he, rather indistinctly because of the sand in his mouth: "Nothing of the kind, greatly respected neighbors. My fall was most beneficial, for it placed me nearly atop my lost shoes. Otherwise I might never have found them." He sobbed to prove his joy.

It is doubtful if the others heard. They, inquisitive fellows that they were, had hands and eyes and tongues busy as they investigated the boat that had caused Chueh Chun's downfall. Lifting a drab and unpromising rain cloth, underneath they discovered a cargo of precious tribute silks—only the best—stuffs such as are sent in tribute to His Majesty, the Emperor. There were bales of silk and sewn garments of silk. There were reds and greens and purples, brown and black and gold. Orange, blue, and pink, they surpassed the rainbow in vivid hue. "How marvelous!" gasped the neighbors. "Your fortune is made, Chueh Chun. What stupendous good luck! We who have always been your truest friends, aiding you with turnips and money in time of need, now rejoice with you."

Chueh Chun nodded. "I must beg leave to disagree on that," was his contradiction. "It is not very good luck. I would sooner have stepped on a fretful tiger. Really, it is terrible—finding this boat."

The neighbors squinted eyes at each other, and spoke: "A pity that you won't take of the find. Howbeit—good for us. We can make profitable use of these things." They were silly to say that.

Chueh Chun promptly loaded his donkey with silks, a burden worth, even in a beggars' market, double or more the thirty thousand cash left by his aunt. He donned a most sightly lilac-colored coat, and departed.

Thus with his donkey laden and his own back resplendent, Chueh Chun faced onward toward Tsun Pu. Scarce had he gone two li when a band of brigands espied him. "There goes old Chueh Chun," said a brigand. "He is too poor to rob. That donkey of his is older than my own dear great-grandfather, and possesses a most deplorable temper." But the robber chief spoke. "Nonsense, you shallow pate. Look at his lilac robe. Look at the silks upon his beast. We could scarcely have better fortune though we opened sacks within our noble Emperor's treasury." So the robbers fell upon Chueh Chun and stripped him of his stuffs. His donkey, his robe, his purse, they took all.

It was a well-plucked traveler who returned to Tien Ting Village and related his misadventure. The villagers, to a man, sympathized greatly. "Our hearts go out to you, most excellent Chueh Chun," they condoled. "Undoubtedly, you have suffered. How you must grieve. And we also grieve. It is all pleasure swept away."

Stubborn Chueh Chun could not agree. Said he: "Who knows but that it was good luck? Had I continued through the mountains, I might have been killed by falling rocks. Think of that. Beyond doubt the robbers saved my life. Yet you, my supposed friends, say it was bad luck."

Early next morning, Chueh Chun's ancient donkey returned to the village. She had broken loose from the brigands and ambled home with all her load of silks intact. How the neighbors rejoiced. A person might easily have thought that the little donkey belonged to them, so jubilant were they. "Oh, Chueh Chun, awake!" they screamed. "Here is your donkey, all hearty and hale—with not so much as a yard of silk missing. What wonderful, wonderful luck!"

Chueh Chun said: "I'm afraid, good gracious yes, it's very bad luck. No good can come of this.

It was a well-plucked traveler who returned.

It's unfortunate as can be. Alas. Alas." Nor was he far wrong. That very morning, while ministering to a wound upon the donkey, that sinful little beast kicked with such violence as to break her master's leg. The somewhat inquisitive neighbors gathered, as bees gather to the blossoming beans. "Oh. Oh. Oh," they screamed. "What is the matter? Did the shameless donkey kick our handsome neighbor?"

"Truly, she did," laughed Chueh Chun. "So hard that I think my leg has come apart." And as he thought, so it was. He could not walk.

The neighbors redoubled their wails, asking each other, "Is not that the extreme height of ill fortune?"

"Not at all," denied old Chueh Chun, perhaps a trifle grumpily. "In my opinion it may be a blessing. It, no doubt, will save me from something worse. Besides, it convinces me that my donkey is very strong, despite her age."

By darkest midnight the Khan of the warlike Tartars, with fifty thousand men, swooped down to raid such villages as had, rather foolishly, been built outside the Great Wall. Tien Ting suffered. Every able-bodied man was taken prisoner. Only the very young, the extremely ancient, the lame, the blind, and the bedridden were left in their homes. Chueh Chun was one of those thus spared. Lameness and age were in his favor. By torchlight a toothless, grinning old neighbor dropped into Chueh Chun's cave to say that the danger was no more. "The Tartars are gone, my admirable friend, Chueh Chun—and so are all of our young men, and our goods, even to house chimneys. I think you and I are about the only ones spared. How fortunate we are!"

"It may be all very fortunate for you," put in Chueh Chun, "but as for me, I have a feeling that things could be much better, and still be not so good. I wish the Tartars had carried me into captivity astride my own poor lost donkey." For, of course, his donkey was gone again.

With the dawning, His Majesty, the Emperor Ching Tang, entered the village to learn of its losses. He was told that all the men, save half a dozen, Chueh Chun among them, had been carried off. "Why wasn't such a one taken?" asked the Emperor. He was told: "A cripple for ninety years and a day." "Why wasn't Chueh Chun taken?" asked the Emperor. "Because, Noble Majesty," answered a villager, kneeling three times and knocking his head on the ground thrice with each kneeling, "because, most gracious light of the sun and beauty of the moon, lord of the earth and sea and sky, Chueh Chun was kicked by his own donkey, and I well remember his saying at the time that it was extremely fortunate his leg was broken—a blessing—those were his words. And they were true."

"What say you?" thundered the Emperor. "A blessing—to be crippled? Why then this Chueh Chun must have known beforehand that the Tartars were coming to carry away my people. He must have known it, and knowing, gave us no warning. Bid this traitorous fellow appear. Soldiers—go. Headsman—draw your sword."

Fortunately, Chueh Chun's wife heard the Emperor's command. Swiftly she ran home. As she entered the cave Chueh Chun sneezed. "Kou Chu." The sneeze led to an excellent idea. Said the wife: "Aha. Aha," with much emphasis. "You were out in your boat on the river last week, and now you have a cold." Adding with proper severity: "Don't you dare go near the river again. Do you hear?" She knew very well what would happen. "My husband—come back."

Lame as he was, Chueh Chun promptly left the cave and got into his boat. The good wife smiled and screamed, "Don't row with such vigor!"

Soldiers ran to the bank of the stream and called, "Come back." And louder they shouted, "Come back!" That was extremely foolish of them. They should have said, "Go on."

Contrary to the last, Chueh Chun sat the wrong way in his boat and rowed for dear life.

Pies of the Princess

Three plump mandarins hid behind a single tiny rosebush. The chancellor crawled under a chair. All courtiers fell upon their chins, and shivering, prayed that soft words might prevail.

For no slight reason did they shiver and hide and pray. King Yang Lang was angry. And he was an old-fashioned Monarch, living in the long ago. Nowadays, any greasy kitchen lout may tweak a King's beard, and go forth to boast of his bravery. But then-a-days, Kings were Kings, and their swords were ever sharp.

King Yang Lang was such a ruler—and more angry than is good to see. His face was purple, and his voice boomed like a battle drum. "Keeper of the Treasury, has all my gold been used to make weights for fishing lines?"

Time after time the treasurer knocked his head against the paving. "Most Glorious and Peaceful Monarch, your gold is so plentiful that seven years must pass before I can finish counting the larger bars—ten years more for the smaller."

That was rather pleasant news. The King's voice lost some of its harshness. "What of ivory? Has all my ivory been burned for firewood, a pot to boil?"

The treasurer continued to knock his head. "Supreme Ruler of the World and the Stars, your ivory completely fills a hundred large and closely guarded vaults."

The King hadn't dreamed that his wealth was so vast. His voice was not more than moderately furious as he asked: "For what reason have you disposed of my jade? Do you mean to say that my jade has been used to build a stable for donkeys?"

Tap, tap, tap, went the treasurer's head on marble paving: "Oh, Powerful Potentate, the store of green jade grows larger each day. Your precious white jade is worth more than green, and gold, and ivory combined. It is all quite safe, under lock and key and watchful spears."

The King was astonished and put in somewhat

better humor. His voice was no louder than thunder as he again questioned the treasurer. "Then why, tell me why is my daughter, the Princess Chin Uor, not given suitable toys. If the treasury holds gold and ivory and jade, why is my daughter compelled to use toys of common clay?"

The treasurer could not explain: "Monarch whose word compels the sun to rise, we have pleaded with the wee Princess Chin Uor. We have given her a thousand dolls of solid gold, with silver cradles for each, cradles set with rubies—and the dolls have eyes of lustrous black pearl. For the princess we have made ivory cats, and ivory mice for the cats to catch—two thousand of each. For the princess we have fashioned, from jade, lovely tossing balls, wonderful dishes, and puppy dogs that bark and come when called. Yet, the princess ignores these things . . . and makes mud pies— Mud Pies. Mightiest Majesty, I do not know why, unless it may be that the princess is a girl, as well as a princess."

A trifle relieved, King Yang Lang passed into the garden. Beside the riverbank he found his daughter, the Princess Chin Uor, or Princess Many Dimples—for that is the meaning of Chin Uor. Nurses standing near kept watch upon wheelbarrows spilling over with golden dolls. But Chin

Uor had no thought for such toys. Her royal hands shaped the tastiest of mud pies. Very pretty pies they were—made of white clay.

The King said: "Littlest and most beautiful daughter, the golden dolls are longing for your touch. Why do you not please them? It is not seemly for a princess to dabble in clay. Then why do you make pies?"

The princess had a very good answer ready. "Because, Daddy, I want to make pies. This nice large one is for your dinner."

The King was so shocked that he could say nothing more. Mud pies for a King's dinner? Such nonsense. His Majesty was scandalized at the thought. He departed in haste.

But the Princess Chin Uor smiled, and kneaded more and more pies. And when she had made enough, she placed them in a wheelbarrow and trundled them to the palace.

And now the story changes. Far away to the west, in a mountain named Huge Rocks Piled, the famous dragon Oo Loong made his home. This fierce dragon was a creature of consuming greed. He was ever hungry and anxious to dine. A rabbit or an elephant—nothing was too large, nothing too small. A turtle or a jellyfish—nothing was too hard, nothing too soft. A man he considered fine

This nice large one is for your dinner.

eating. Boys he liked somewhat better. Girls? Girls were far superior to boys—in the dragon's opinion.

Much sorrow this ferocious *loong* had created in His Majesty's kingdom. A reward of one hundred silver pieces had been offered for the dragon's horns, two hundred for his ears. Magicians had worked charms to slay him—only themselves to be slain. Hunters had loaded their jingals with yellow paper, and had fired where the dragon was thickest, fired where he was thinnest—only to be eaten —their guns with them. Made angry by the loss of so many people, King Yang Lang marched an army into the Mountain of Huge Rocks Piled. And the army was well armed with thumping drums and fifes and smoking guns.

Then the dragon became doubly furious and ferocious. To punish King Yang Lang, he resolved to visit the palace. That, he knew, would cause the army to be withdrawn. Accordingly, at the hour of deepest slumber, darksome mid of night, he prowled round Yang Lang's palace, seeking entrance. He had no easy task. Upon the King's door were pictures, also the word "Chi," written in gold. And so that door was well protected. The Queen's door likewise was dragonproof. It was covered with whole sentences taken from the black book of Hu Po, master magician. The door that led to where Princess Chin Uor slept was made strong by magic words and symbols. More of Hu Po's sorcery. Useless to prowl there. Dangerous to prowl there. The dragon was a knowing beast, and prudent. The signs were against him. Hence, he tarried not, but crawled down the hallway in leaving.

A wheelbarrow stood in his path. He could not pass to the right. To the left he could not pass. Nor could he leap over the obstruction. But the dragon was not one to be baffled by such a weak and wooden contrivance. His huge mouth opened and his white-hot breath rushed forth. In a twinkling the wooden barrow vanished. Like a butter cake dropped upon the summer sun, it melted, burned to a cinder of nothingness.

Now the wheelbarrow thus destroyed was property of the little Princess Chin Uor. In it had been golden dolls, dolls of the princess. The dolls were dolls no longer. Under the dragon's fiery breath they changed to a pool of liquid gold. The hard gold became soft and flowing.

In the barrow had been pretty mud pies, pies of the princess. Under the dragon's burning breath they were changed to disks of stony hardness. The soft clay took on a hardness as of flint. The princess had wished her pies to dry. And her wish had been granted.

Next morning, the palace, from presence room to pantry, buzzed with excitement. Oo Loong had dared intrude within the royal dwelling. It could not be doubted. He had left his footprints in the molten gold, and the gold, in hardening, had preserved his tracks.

Witches and wizards came to make more able charms. Messengers galloped away to summon the distant army. The King raged and roared. Said His Majesty: "Let that reprobate dragon return, if he dares. If he dares, let that reprobate dragon return." The courtiers trembled and gasped: "Pray may the wicked *loong* never return. Never, never return." But little Princess Many Dimples played with her pies, and was happy. Her pies had been baked to a queen's taste—or rather to the taste of a princess. Beside the river she worked faithfully in wet white clay. Such beautiful pies. "I do hope that the nice *loong* will return," said Princess Chin Uor. "He is such a fine oven. I shall make a hundred more pies for his baking."

Pie after pie. Even the nurses helped. Instead of saying, "Please, will your Royal Highness not play with this lovely doll?" they said, "Please, is this one rounded enough?" and "Please, shall I scallop the edges a trifle deeper?" and "Shall I imagine that this one contains cherries or radishes?" or whatever it may be that makers of pies would say in a royal kitchen. So, a hundred pies were made and wheeled to the palace. In reality, they numbered a hundred and one, but the odd one was so thick that it must be called a cake. Howbeit, that is not so important as you might think.

Night followed day—a habit that most nights have. The soldiers slept—as they had been ordered not to do. The hour approached when clock hands point to the highest sky. Midnight came, and with it the mountainous mountain *loong*. Unseen by those whose duty was seeing, the dragon entered King Yang Lang's courtyard. And there he was perplexed and paused. The King's door was a hodgepodge of magic signs, plastered with yellow paper. Vain to think of entering there. The Queen's door was upside down—best charm of all. To think of entering was vain. The door that led to Princess Chin Uor's sleeping chamber was written thick with words to still a dragon's heart, circles to dizzy his head. Say what you please, the witches and wizards had done good work upon that door. Their charms were written with clearness and force. The *loong* dared not take a second glance. He felt his limbs grow weak. Wisely hastened he from the spell-guarded threshold.

Now, in the reign of the Emperor Ming, a crazed and knavish fellow, known to the world as Wing Dow, invented a contrivance called by him "Look-through-the-wall," but which we of today call a "window." His invention gave the Emperor Ming a severe cold, and Wing Dow came within a sword's width of losing his ears—but more of that later. Here it is necessary to say only that Look-through-the-walls became popular, and many such were to be found in King Yang Lang's palace. In the Princess Chin Uor's room were many wing-dows (or windows), and—hard to believe—those wing-dows were unguarded either by charm or by apple-wood beam, which is as good as a charm. Could the dragon pass by such a fine chance? Could he pass the wing-dow and not have a try? When he had come with purpose to do harm? It is easy to imagine the thing that happened. And yet not so easy as may seem.

The dragon's lumpish head entered the wing-dow. His deer horns, his rabbit eyes, his snake tongue, all entered, and easily enough. A ponderous sofa-cushion foot he placed upon the window ledge. . . .

Crash, and smash, and clatter . . .

The nurses awoke and screamed, "Save us!"

The Princess Chin Uor awoke and said, "Shoo."

Soldiers in the courtyard awoke and lighted

green fires as they smote their drums, saying:
"Come if you dare. Help. Help."

The dragon was already awake—awake to the
danger. Promptly he vanished. Such noise he could
not abide.

King Yang Lang came with a golden torch.
Greatly he was pleased that the *loong* had been
routed.

But Princess Chin Uor was far from pleased.
Indeed, she was fretful. From the floor she took a
sliver of flint-hard clay. "My pies are all broken.
All. All are broken," mourned Princess Many
Dimples. "I had placed them in the wing-dow. And
the dragon knocked them down and broke them."
And beyond doubt so had he done. There were the
pieces.

Still the King remained cheerful. His little
daughter's sadness passed unnoticed. His Majesty
said: "Your pies, my daughter, are excellent food
—let no one deny it—but even better are they to
give warning of the dragon's nearness. Your pies
have provided me with a wonderful idea. Here-
after we need have no more fear of the *loong*. . . .
Ho. General. Awaken your soldiers again. Let
them march to the river."

For a week the King's army did no other labor
than make mud pies. And liked it. The pies were

given heat in giant ovens, were baked into stony hardness. Then they were placed throughout the palace, in windows, upon tables, chairs, upon chests and shelves, high and low and everywhere. Even on the chimney tops were rows of glistening pies. The slightest misstep by a prowling dragon would have caused a din most tremendous.

The royal dining table was a shining whiteness, covered with mud pies. So numerous were the pies of the princess that no room remained for food. But that was no cause for worry. The King merely ordered that his rice be placed upon a baked clay pie. Mandarins who visited the palace were much surprised at what they saw—a King eating from common clay. Nevertheless, their own tables were soon covered with Princess Chin Uor's pies. For the King, of course, set all fashions.

And so, we modern peoples speak of our plates and cups and saucers as "China." China? Is it? Yes, and no. China is merely our way of pronouncing Chin Uor. Our plates are merely thin copies of Princess Chin Uor's pies.

As Hai Low Kept House

After weary years of saving, a few cash each calendar, Hai Lee removed from the mountains, where nothing ever happens, and bought a tiny house that stood near Ying Ling toll road, which is the King's road, and where strange sights are seen. In that region the people have a saying, "He who lives on the King's road has seen the whole world."

With him the newcomer brought his little brother, Hai Low. Hai Low was to keep house, while Hai Lee worked in field and forest. The new house was no larger than two by twice, and poorly furnished. Nevertheless, Hai Lee and Hai Low imagined it to be grand. For they had always lived in a mountain cave.

Many times Hai Lee cautioned his brother to

take good care that no harm came to their magnificent house. And Hai Low promised faithfully to guard. His eyes would be unblinkingly open. Have no fear.

Upon the very first day, as Hai Low kept house, a fox dashed under the flooring. A band of hunters soon appeared. The hunters said, "We hope you enjoyed a tasty dinner." That by way of greeting. "Our fox has hidden beneath your house. He is a very damage-doing fox, and we desire his ears. For permission to dig we will thank you a thousand times—and more if the fur be of good quality."

Hai Low thought of his brother's warning. Whereupon he replied to the hunters: "Your digging might injure the house, and my honorable brother has told me to keep all harm away. Therefore, excellent huntsmen, I must, in sorrow, give you no. Dig you cannot, for the house might fall."

With soft voices the hunters wheedled. Hai Low said no. With harsh voices the hunters blustered and threatened. Hai Low said no. Money the hunters offered. Hai Low said no. His mind was fixed, and nothing could move it. No once. No twice. No thrice. And again no. The hunters departed. The fox remained. And Hai Low believed he had done well for his first day of housekeeping.

He imagined that his brother would praise him.

The opposite came to pass. Hai Lee frowned. "That was wrong and stupidly done, Small Brother. A little digging could have given no hurt. The fox is an evil enemy. He will catch all of our fowls, even to the last speckled hen. We must get rid of that scamp. If any more hunters come—tell them to dig."

Upon the next day, as Hai Low kept house, he beheld two men with crossbows. In joy he rushed to greet them. With much bowing and scraping he said: "I hope that your rice was well cooked, and you had plenty of it. Will you not come to the house and dig?"

One of the men said, "This fellow reminds me of the way Wu Ta Lang got out of the cherry tree—it was quite simple." But the other, who was more crafty, squinted an eye to say, "Be quiet." Then, using his tongue, he spoke to Hai Low: "For nothing else we came. With all our hearts will we dig. Only open the door. Our rice was well cooked." He entered the house and began to tear up stones from the hearth. Hai Low said, "Do you not think the fox will be alarmed and try to escape through the hole by which he entered?" The hunter replied: "A wise question, truly. What shall we do? Can you not sit with your back to the entrance? Then the fox will be unable to depart." Hai Low readily agreed to aid. He went outside and sat with his back to the wall. The hunters struck many blows upon the hearth, laughing all the while. Presently each said, "Oh," and stopped digging. "Have you got it?" asked Hai Low. "We have," the elder huntsman answered. "We have it in a sack. How fortunate that you invited us in! Our digging was most successful." He was greatly pleased. The other hunter seemed equally pleased. Hai Low, too, was delighted. A very fine thing he thought it that the fox had been captured. He felt sure that his brother would speak words of praise.

But such was far from being. Hai Lee tossed a sack upon the table and said: "Oh, my little Brother, a sad mistake you made this day. Not hunters, but thieves were those men. Not a fox, but all of our money they carried off in the sack. By chance alone, I regained it. But such good luck rarely happens a second time. Now heed my words. Never again permit strangers to enter the house. Never."

Next day, as Hai Low kept house, the door shook with a great knocking. They boy peeped from a window. He beheld an old man, beating the door. Said Hai Low: "I hope you relished your dinner—but you must go away. My brother says that I am to admit no strangers. Go away. You cannot enter."

The old man remarked, in a loud tone, that Hai Low spoke nonsense. "Open the door that I may enter, you who deserve a bamboo upon your back. Is this any way to treat your own flesh and blood?" Hai Low repeated his command. "You cannot enter. Go away hurriedly—else I shall pour hot water." He tilted a kettle and began to pour. Whereupon the old man took to his heels, for the water steamed, hot from a fire. Hai Low was well pleased with himself. Beyond doubt, he would receive great praise from his brother.

But Hai Lee came home in a huff. Angry, dismayed, was the big brother. "Oh, you wrong-doing little Brother, you have ruined our future. The man whom you chased away was Grandfather Hai Ho, wealthy and about to make us his heirs. Now he says he will leave us not so much as one cash, not one. For pity's sake, small Brother, be more tactful. We have another rich grandfather. When the next stranger comes, ask him if he is your grandfather, before you pour heated water."

Next day, as Hai Low kept house, the door rattled and banged. Someone wished to come in. At least, it seemed probable. Hai Low peered from a window. He beheld a man, well dressed and round, at the door. Behind the impatient one were many slaves. At once Hai Low thought of his other rich grandfather. Said he: "I hope your rice was served on a golden dish. Are you my grandfather?"

"What?" roared the stranger. "What? What impudence were you saying?" Hai Low used a full breath to shout, "I asked, are you my grandfather. MY GRANDFATHER." At that the large stranger tottered. His slaves made a tremendous breeze with fans, seeking to revive him. Still fanning, they carried him away. Hai Low was somewhat puzzled. And puzzled he remained until his brother came home.

The brother was frightened, likewise angry. "Oh, dear me, small Brother, why were you so rude to the Governor? You have insulted the Governor, and will be lucky if you escape with your life. Even if you are not beheaded, you will have to pay a fine of a thousand large coins. All because of your foolish questions. I beseech you, don't ask visitors any more questions. Don't open your mouth to a stranger."

Next day, as Hai Low kept house, he chanced to glance at the stable. The stable door was open. Before the boy could close it, a stranger came out, leading Hai Lee's fine donkey. Hai Low began to imagine that mischief was being done. Thrice he opened his mouth, but each time he remembered his brother's instruction to ask no questions. So he remained silent. The donkey was soon saddled. Away it went, with the stranger astride.

When big brother returned home for Evening Rice, he spoke harshly to Hai Low. "Goodness, gracious me, very small Brother, you will ruin us yet. Now you've let a rogue take my trotting donkey, and only by a lucky accident was I able to recover the beast. Really, your housekeeping is a bad thing altogether. Never let another stranger approach the stable. He might take our milking cow. If another stranger goes near the stable— shoot him."

Next day, as Hai Low kept house, he sat upon the door step. In his hand he clenched a bow. Again and again he glanced toward the stable. No person should take the milking cow. Not without regret. Beware, rogues, or suffer.

A traveler came down the road. He was a rich man and wore a hat that was high and covered with feathers. It was such a hat as the wind demons love for a toy. A sudden breeze lifted the traveler's hat and whirled it fast and far. It came to earth in front of the stable. Of course, the stranger followed it, running, to the stable door.

Hai Low remembered his brother's command. He made a V of the bowstring. His hurried arrow went seeking a mark. The traveler gave up all thought of recovering his hat. Down the road he dashed madly, shouting that he had been killed. However, he was a traveler, and travelers are noted for stories hard to believe. Hai Low sat on the steps and had practice with his bow. No man should take the milking cow, without taking an arrow also. A thief had best wear clothes of iron.

When Big Brother Hai Lee came home, his voice was doleful. "Oh, Brother, my Brother, you have put us into vast trouble. Why on earth did you shoot an arrow into the traveler's quilted coat? He is a foreign ambassador, and says that his country will instantly declare war upon us. Think of the sadness your act will cause. I beg of you be not so rash in future. The next time you see a stranger lose his hat, don't shoot. Instead, be polite, and chase the hat."

Next day, as Hai Low kept house, he noticed a great company of men approaching. Gong beaters led. Behind them came carriers of banners; tablet men; keepers of the large umbrellas; warriors; more gong musicians; fan carriers; incense swingers—a long procession it was. Hai Low knew that it must be the marching train of a truly great

He made a V of the bowstring.

man. He hoped that he might behold the high and mighty one. And so he did. As the gilded sedan chair was borne past, a breeze threshed its curtains. A hat soared out of the sedan. Carried by the wind demons, it rolled across turnip patch and radish. Hai Low dashed away in chase. He thought himself being polite and useful—to rescue the great one's hat.

Alas, a hundred bludgeon men and spear wavers rushed after him. They shouted that he must stop and be killed for his sin. Hai Low had no idea why they wished to slay him. Neither had he the faintest idea of stopping. He lifted his heels with such rapidity that he gained a thicket three leaps ahead of the foremost warrior men. In the heavy growth of briers and bushes he was safe, for he knew the tangle in all its winding ways. To follow was folly.

When late, the boy reached home, he found his brother waiting. Hai Lee's despair was shown in tears and quavering words. "Oh, Brother of mine, I fear that your life is worth less than a withered carrot. Why did you lay hands upon His Majesty's right royal hat? Do you not know that death is the penalty for so doing? Soldiers have sought you high and low. If they find you—I cannot bear to say what will happen. Now please have regard for my words, little Brother. Go into the house, and crawl under a bed—and stay there. Stay there.''

Next day, as Hai Low kept house, he kept it beneath a bed. So still he lay that a mouse took a nap at his side. Soldiers came and emptied the pantry, eating and drinking as only King's men can. None of them thought to glance under the bed. And that was just as well—just as well for Hai Low. It was for him that they had come to search.

Soon after the soldiers had departed, an odor of burning filled the air. The house was afire. Hai Low coughed, but he dared not crawl from his shielding bed. He had no doubt the fire had been set in an effort to rout him from hiding.

The door flew open and in rushed big brother Hai Lee. Hai Lee flung water upon the flames, then pulled little brother from beneath the bed. He was greatly exasperated. ''My word and all, not very large Brother, would you let the house burn and not fling a bucket? The soldiers were gone. Why didn't you arise and douse the flames? Now hear what I speak, little Brother. The next time you see flames—pour on water. Pour on water.''

Next day, as Hai Low kept house, he chanced to gaze down the road. A brisk fire burned in the open. With two filled buckets the boy hastened to obey his brother's order. In no time he wetted the fire out of burning.

Scarce had he entered the house when Big Brother Hai Lee entered. Hai Lee had his tongue on edge for scolding. "My very own Brother, why must you be always at mischief? What in all the green earth and the blue sky made you throw water upon that fire? A traveler was boiling his rice—and you with water put out his fire. It was outrageous. Now then, to atone for your impishness, take this stick of dry wood to the traveler so that he can boil his rice. And, as you give him the stick, be sure to apologize. Ask for pardon."

Away went Hai Low at his fastest, bearing a huge bamboo. The traveler beheld him, and promptly mounted a horse. Many robbers made misery in that region. The traveler had gained saddening experience of them. He imagined that Hai Low must be a robber—else why did the fellow wave a long bamboo? So the traveler put heels to his horse, and galloped. But Hai Low was not to be left far behind. He followed swiftly, shouting words that mean stop, wait, hold on, tarry. And the more he shouted, the more determined grew the traveler never to stop until he had found protection in a camp of soldiers.

Several young men let curiosity lead them to follow Hai Low. They wished to discover why he pursued the traveler. As they raced through a village, other men joined. Another village gave a dozen more. A town furnished twice as many. Soon Hai Low had an enormous crowd at his heels. Dust hung above in a blinding curtain. The trample of feet and the excited shouts could be heard for distant miles. More dust and more, more men and more. At first they asked, "What's it all about?" Later, "Catch him," and "Kill him," they cried.

Hai Low had long since lost sight of the fast fleeing horseman. But he reasoned that the traveler would enter Ying Ling, the capital city. Hence, he too, leading his curious host, entered Ying Ling. He was determined to do as his brother had bidden.

Now it chanced that King How Wang was a most unpopular ruler. Threats had been made against him. A prince from the north was said to be raising an army of rebels. Hence, when King How Wang beheld Hai Low's approach at the head of a vast army, he imagined Hai Low to be the northern prince. Hai Low's curious rabble he thought a rebel army. So thinking, he called for his horse. . . . And what became of him no one can say. He vanished, for good and all.

The royal generals, instead of ordering a fight, promptly knelt before Hai Low and bumped their heads in the dust. Said they, "We bow unto our

*The royal generals . . . knelt before Hai Low and
bumped their heads in the dust.*

new King." The palace soldiers said, "Hail to our
new King." And the breathless mob shouted,
"Long live our new King." The crown was placed
upon astonished Hai Low's head. The mace of
authority was placed in his hand. And "Hail," and
"Hail," and "Hail."

Thus did Hai Low, in chase of an unknown
traveler, become King upon a throne. His days of
housekeeping were ended. And so is the book . . .
ended.